I0451227

CHRISTMAS HAVEN

A Sweet Christmas Volume 9

SAMANTHA JACOBEY

Lavish
Publishing LLC

First Edition

A Sweet Christmas Series Book 9

2023 Lavish Publishing, LLC

All Rights Reserved

Published in the United States by Lavish Publishing, LLC, Midland, TX

Cover Design by: Victor R. Sosa

Cover Images: CanStock

Paperback Edition

ISBN: 978-1-64900-065-1

www.LavishPublishing.com

Contents

Prologue

From her bed, Candy glared at the clock on the small table next to her head. *Damn. The alarm won't go off for half an hour*, she mentally calculated. *Maybe I can get a little more sleep. It's graduation day, after all.*

But she wouldn't. She could already feel the weight of their situation pressing down on her, and her final completion of school did not ring with the satisfaction she had hoped it would. Rolling onto her back, she sniffed into the darkness.

"You ok?" Gary muttered.

"Yeah," she croaked.

He pushed up to lean on an elbow and stared at her silhouette. "Just breathe, Kitten. She's still here." He took a stab at the cause of her distress knowing it could be any number of things.

"Yup," she bit tartly. "They gave her six months. Just in time for Christmas."

Not really happy with hitting the target, he extended his free hand to lovingly caress her cheek with the backs of his fingers. "We knew it was coming," he soothed. "Enjoy her while you can, love."

Candy blinked rapidly, a squeal tightening her throat. Turning, she buried her face in his chest. "It should be a happy day. Days. I'm finally done. And the house is nearly finished, too. We'll be ready to bring in some girls before the summer is over, but how can I think about it? How can I focus on anything knowing how soon I'm going to lose her?"

Candy's mother had been ill most of her life. She had fought hard, but this latest blow had cut the deepest; the pronouncement of an ending almost more than she could take.

Gary firmly massaged her shoulder and back. "You'll manage. Besides, you four girls are a team. I'm sure your first tenants will be well cared for even when you need to focus on your mother." He smiled at the thought of the rooms they were converting. "It makes her proud to see your accomplishments."

Stifling a sob, she clung to him, considering the notion. "And today. She'll get to see me walk the stage." She hadn't thought of that. Her father had missed it all, being taken so long ago. Fighting to sit up, she wiped at her damp lashes. "You're right. I should be thankful for all those things. All the time we've had with her."

"That's the spirit," he agreed. Sitting up beside her, he leaned over to nuzzle her with a brief kiss on her temple, then slid smoothly off his side of the bed.

Silently, Candy watched him disappear into their bathroom. She needed to put on a brave face, especially now. Her mother's health had been on a slow decline for years, but she had been diagnosed with terminal cancer only the week before. She should cherish her for as many days as she could. But in the end, she knew she had always been right about her least favorite holiday.

Christmas has always been hard for me, she lamented, giving herself a hug. *And this one just might do me in*. There was no silver lining this year. *This will either be my last Christmas with my mother, or my first one without her*.

Flopping over onto the mattress, she threw the comforter over her head. She needed to be strong and dependable for everyone's sake. However, she could linger in her sorrow for another twenty-three minutes if she wanted to.

ONE

Best Laid Plans

"I'll meet you over at the house, unless you call to tell me it's a bust," Carol practically sang as Candy prepared to leave.

Her employer forced a smile. "That's optimistic. We aren't even sure she'll be a good fit."

"I can't wait to meet her!" Holly chimed in from Lanelle's adjoining suite.

"We have faith in your assessment," their nanny seconded briskly. "You can call and let me know, but otherwise I'm going over to make a room ready in about an hour."

"Ok, if you don't hear from me, then you can expect us," Candy reluctantly agreed. Pausing at the back door, she listened to the activity in her mother's bedroom, then called, "I'll be back soon," to the rest of the Ford household.

"No rush," Holly replied through the wall once more.

Candice managed to smile and nod to the girl at the sink before closing the portal behind her. The prospect of their first client had everyone in an excited mood, despite her own trepidation.

Crossing the yard, she climbed into her little blue Prius and tossed her purse into the passenger seat. Turning onto the street, her mind wandered back to her making the same drive five years prior nearly to the day. *The day we got Joylana*, she reminisced.

Making her way through the early December traffic, she thought about Glenda's call. "Why didn't I just tell her no?" she asked herself sternly. No one else would have been the wiser. "Because we can't hold out any longer," she grunted a moment later, her thoughts drawn to the large house across the street from her own.

Originally, the four women had intended to start taking on boarders as soon as the first two rooms had been converted. However, those plans had been laid aside after Lanell's diagnosis. Instead, they had finished the privacy suite for Holly, Caroline and Grace. Then they had put time into each of the five bedrooms with full baths, completing each as a small one-room apartment. The three remaining bedrooms had also been converted, one into a kitchen and one a family room that would be shared by their tenants as common rooms. The remaining and least desirable bedroom had been subdivided into five large closets complete with locking doors for storage, one for each guest.

Gary and Ben had lent a hand with the most strenuous renovations, and they had taken their time, moving from project to project. Eventually they had run out of things to do.

"We're stalling," Candy admitted as she waited at a red light. The halfway house had been finished for months, but with Lanelle's condition on everyone's mind, no one had been in a hurry to take on their first client. Candy sighed, knowing they wouldn't be taking one now if Glenda hadn't insisted it was urgent.

Parking in front of the older woman's office, Candy braced herself against the chill wind and hurried inside.

"Good afternoon!" Glenda's secretary greeted her. "Is it snowing yet?"

"No," Candice groused, glancing around the empty chairs that lined the lobby. "But it's awfully gray, so it might. I love a white Christmas as much as the next person, but with over two weeks to go, it's way too early for it!"

"It's never too early for snow," Glenda Tucker countered from her door. "You can come in."

Stepping into the small space, Candy rubbed her hands together, then pulled at her gloves to remove them. "I thought I would meet her," she chirped as she observed the office was unoccupied as well.

"You will," Glenda explained. "I thought it would be best if we spoke for a moment before you do."

"Oh. When is she due?" Candy asked. Perching on the edge of a plush chair, she shoved the coverings into a pocket and opened her notebook. "I've prepared an intake form so I can have all the particulars." She held up the pages as evidence.

"Candice, I must apologize." The woman behind the desk anxiously adjusted herself in her seat. "I didn't want to give you too many details over the phone, and now that the moment is at hand, I find myself feeling a little guilty."

Candy gaped at her in surprise. Her brow crinkled, she gasped, "Are we not getting a client from you?"

"Oh, you are. But first, I want you to know that you can decline. This would be a huge favor for me. And to Michelle. And maybe even to you, as I understand you don't have any clients yet. This just might be the push you need to get moving. But I don't want you to feel pressured to do this," Glenda explained.

Too late, Candy silently mused, pursing her lips. Aloud she replied, "Well, I'm here to assess whether we can help. Tell me about her, and we'll go from there."

"Michelle isn't pregnant, Candy." Glenda tapped the flat surface before her with her nails. "She's in the process of transitioning."

"Transitioning." Candy stared at her. "Transitioning," she repeated. That word should mean something, but for the life of her she couldn't think of what.

"Michelle was born a man. Michael," Glenda offered. "But please don't call her that."

The color drained from Candy's features. "We have rooms for unwed mothers," she managed. "We can't have a man living there."

Glenda folded her hands in front of her as she scooted up to her desk. Sitting up straight, she inhaled a slow, cleansing breath. "I know this is a shock. And I wouldn't ask if I thought there would be a problem. But as I said, I understood you haven't accepted anyone yet."

"No, this is our first." Feeling heavy, Candy's body drooped. Holding up her pen and spiral, she groaned, "I don't know about this. The apartments are furnished for families. Small children and babies. I don't even know what to say." She dropped her appendages onto her lap, feeling helpless.

Raising her chin, Glenda smiled at her. "I knew it would be a shock. That's why I wanted to give us a minute to talk before you meet her."

The color returned to Candy's cheeks as a hot flush. "Why do I need to meet her? This isn't what we're looking for," she stammered.

"She needs you," Glenda insisted. "Please. Allow me to

introduce you. You can interview her. I know you have a good heart, Candice. All you need now is an open mind. Give her a few minutes before you turn her away." Standing, she didn't wait for a reply and simply opened the door to her right, which led to a smaller, private waiting area.

That's why I didn't see her when I came in. Feeling manipulated, Candy scowled, unable to hide her displeasure. Her eyes meeting Michelle's, she noted the defiance behind them. Dropping her gaze, she started at the dirty white sneakers and combed her way up to the slender face. On the way, she noted the jeans and blouse were only an adequate fit, and were largely hidden by an oversized hoodie that hung about her slender frame.

At the top, the young woman wore no makeup and her dark hair had been ironed flat and greased so that it stuck straight down around her neck, barely scraping her shoulders. "I'm Michelle Miller." Stepping forward, the girl offered her hand stiffly.

"Candice Ford." Candy accepted the appendage, staring at it as their skin touched. Her thoughts jumbled, she marveled at the smallness of it. "You're not very big," she blurted, managing to stop there.

Shocked, Michelle pulled her fingers away and tugged her jacket closed across her flat chest.

"No, I meant your hand." Candy's flush deepened. "Oh God, how rude of me." She licked her lips, then indicated the second chair. "We should sit."

Michelle cut her annoyed gaze over at Glenda. "Is this the best you can do?"

"Have a seat," Glenda urged. "I know this is hard for you. Neither of you are getting what you expected, but that doesn't mean it won't work."

Tightening her jaw, Michelle accepted the cushion. "What do you want to know?"

Unsure where to begin, Candy stared at her prepared script. "Your name is Michelle Miller," she stated as she wrote it across the top of the first page. "How old are you?"

"Twenty-seven."

Candy's fingers gripped the pen tightly as she added the notes. "Why are you in need of assistance?"

"Because my family don't want me to do this." Her voice crisp, Michelle bit her lip to stop the tremor.

Candy scrawled, then looked at the hands clasped in the lap beside her. "How long have you wanted to be a woman?"

"When I was ten, I promised myself." She stopped short and a few of the slender fingers swiped a tear from her face. "I told myself I would do whatever it takes."

Lifting her eyes slowly, Candy met the mahogany-colored orbs. The damp cheek a soft, creamy brown, she thought of her ebony princess. "Is there anyone in your family who supports you?" she almost whispered.

"Nope." Alone in her fight, the word cut clean through the air and the pucker of Michelle's lips punctuated it perfectly.

Candy inhaled deeply. Shifting her attention to Glenda, she nodded. "We'll take her. I may have to do some convincing, though. This isn't exactly what we had in mind."

"Don't do me any favors," Michelle snapped. "I don't need 'em."

"Michelle, we talked about this," Glenda countered firmly. "You need support."

Candy smiled, sensing an invisible connection between them. She had been the same surly girl not so long ago. "We are almost the same age," she offered quietly.

"And?" Michelle folded her arms in front of her.

"And I just finished school this last spring. I'm starting a new chapter in my life. And it appears that you are, too."

"I guess," her new client grunted.

Accepting that they would need a period of adjustment, Candy closed her book. "How do we do this?" She looked at Glenda for guidance.

"Well, we have her bag in the other room if you're prepared to take her with you," the social worker offered. She casually indicated the small chamber on the other side of the wall. "Or I can put her up again tonight. In that case, I'll bring her over to the house tomorrow."

"Tonight will be fine," Candy agreed, noting the look of disappointment on her new charge's strained features.

TWO

Homecoming

Candy took the return trip in a rather roundabout route, giving the girls a few minutes for unsupervised conversation. "What can you tell me about yourself?" she asked, hoping for a friendly tone.

"Not much." Michelle stared out of the passenger side window, not looking at her new host. "Where are we going, anyways?"

"We're going to the house. You'll be staying with Holly, Carol and Grace, their daughter." Candy paused, giving her words time to sink in before she continued.

"Their daughter?" Michelle's dark features swung around to glare at her. "You're kidding me."

"Not at all." Candy chuckled. "Michelle dear, you are through the looking glass. Our family is anything but ordinary. Hopefully, you will feel at ease among our brand of chaos." She grinned, realizing why Glenda had called her. Nothing in their bubble could be considered conventional. It was only natural to have someone transitioning under their supervision. "Should I tell you about everyone, or would you like to be surprised?"

"I'll be surprised if we ever get there," Michelle clipped. "We just came from that way." She pointed at a cross street, indicating they appeared to be lost.

"I thought we might need a few minutes," Candy explained nonchalantly. "Would you like to stop for anything?" She eyed the backpack in the passenger floorboard with suspicion. "Perhaps a few personal items to make you more comfortable."

Her dark eyes following her gaze, Michelle shrugged. "Not yet. I need to figure some things out before I go buying stuff."

Candy nodded, making another turn and pointing the car towards home. "We'll help you with that. How long have you lived as a woman?"

Michelle shrugged. "Not long. I never had girl's clothes before, but Glenda gave me these. I like them."

"I see." Candy grimaced, bracing herself in case there was a tantrum. "I assume you don't have your own place. Were you living with your parents, or maybe a sibling, before you told them? A lover maybe?" Her voice trailed away, as she could guess forever and not get it right without help, so she hoped the prod would be enough.

Michelle exhaled a loud sigh. "Yeah, I stay with my family. My sister is married to some white guy, and I stay with them sometimes, too. But all my stuff is at my parents' place. When they found out I was gonna transition, they told me I couldn't come in their house to get it." She turned back to the window, sulking. "They can keep it."

Candy winced. "We'll find a way to retrieve your things."

"It don't matter. I need new stuff anyways," Michelle observed quietly, sounding defeated.

On their street, Candice grew tense as she approached the houses that faced one another. Taking the right-hand drive, she pulled up next to the girls' patio and cut off the engine. "Don't go yet. I need to tell you something first."

"What?" Michelle stared at the giant house next to them.

"I know things are hard. And they may not be what you want every day. Even most days. But that doesn't mean it won't get better, so hang in there." Candy fought the urge to hug her and settled for giving her a quick pat on the leg. "We're here to help you."

Michelle slowly drew her eyes away from the massive dwelling to face her. "Glenda said you was a good person, with a good heart. Are they good people, too?"

Candy gasped. "How did you know? You weren't even in the room yet!"

"I was listening," Michelle confessed meekly. She cupped her ear with her hand, mimicking the closed door. "I didn't like feeling like she was hiding me."

Candy grimaced, aware that Glenda had in fact done exactly that. "She wanted to prepare me, that's all," Candy assured. "Come on. I promise, you'll be welcome here."

Climbing out, Candy met Michelle at the base of the steps and led her to the sliding glass door where Caroline stood waiting. She could tell by the look on the taller girl's face that she had a lot of explaining to do, but when the portal opened her friend appeared at ease.

"Who do we have here?" Carol asked casually, stepping back to allow them inside.

Crossing the threshold, the aroma of a homecooked meal calmed Candy's tension. "This is Michelle," she offered. "She's twenty-seven and in the process of transitioning."

"Ok, then we can either leave the crib, or wheel it down to the storage. Is that all you have?" Caroline indicated the girl's pack with a limp hand.

"Yeah, I ain't got nothing else." Michelle glanced at Candy and inhaled deeply. "Look, I don't need a handout. This all took me by surprise, that's all. I got a job and a bank account. I just don't have my stuff, or a place to stay. I wasn't really ready for it all to go down like it did."

"Do you have a car?" Carol asked doubtfully, discreetly looking her up and down as she moved about her kitchen to complete their evening meal.

"No. I'm saving all my money for my surgeries. I wanna get tops and bottoms, and that costs, you know?" Michelle noticed Grace in her highchair at the table and extended a single digit towards her in greeting. "Are we having supper?"

"We are as soon as Holly gets home," Carol explained. "You know, your room is open and ready if you want to go freshen up. You have a bathroom and everything. You can't miss it. Just look for the big red three on the door, and your keys are lying on the dresser. Room key, front door, and storage closet." Her smile bright, she indicated the stairs as she spoke.

"All right, I'll be back down in a minute." Slinking past them, Michelle clomped up the stairs noisily.

"Are you crazy?" Carol hissed as soon as she disappeared, the grin gone. "We can't have a transvestite living here!"

"She's transitioning, so I don't think that's the same thing," Candy snipped. Opening the fridge, she fished out her bottle of wine. "You want some?" she asked, filling a small glass.

"Explain, Candy. Now. Holly will be home any minute, and you know she is going to flip out. She was so looking forward to this!"

"I don't think it will be that bad." Candy shrugged, sipping her beverage. "You guys are lesbians, after all."

"Not funny," Carol groaned. "I thought we were doing pregnant girls who need help getting on their feet."

"Well, we seem to be all out of those," Candy teased. "What we have now is a young man who wants to be a woman." She grinned. "I was floored myself when Glenda told me, but then I met her. Honestly, I think we can really help her."

"What makes you think that?" Carol grunted. She turned to the stove and blended one of the pots furiously.

"Well, she said her parents told her she couldn't go home when they found out. I didn't get much further than that," Candy confessed, her expression slipping into dolefulness. "She's lost, Carol. We do lost."

Caroline paused her stirring and sighed. "Yeah, I guess we do. But you should go break it to Holly, so she has a chance to calm down before she gets over here. I'll go up and check on her here in a sec. Michelle you said?"

"Yes." Candy toasted her friend and polished off her drink. "I'll go prepare her, and you guys call me if you need anything during the night." Placing her glass in the sink, Candy waved at Grace, who still sat contentedly gnawing her banana, then slid the glass door shut behind her on the way out.

THREE

What You Ask For

"Hey!" Holly chirped as Candy entered the kitchen through the back door a short time later. "Is she getting settled?"

Catching pure excitement in her voice, Candice cringed. "She is, but we need to talk before you head over there." She paused, smiling down at her mother, who sat at the table in her favorite chair. "Are you feeling nosey or hungry?"

"Both," Lanelle rasped.

"I see." Candy chuckled. She inspected the large pot of stew Carol had left on the stove for them, then retrieved a small bowl from the cabinet.

"Don't keep me waiting," Holly teased, all but ready to leave.

Serving the dish with warm broth and bits of vegetables, Candy could hear her children playing down the hall in the den. On the other side of the wall, in the living room, her husband stoked and fed the fire.

"Candy!" Holly insisted, relieving her of the bowl and placing it before Lanelle.

Ignoring her, Candy sidled over to the large doorway that connected the two rooms and addressed her spouse. "Are you ready to eat?"

His stomach rumbling, Gary considered the offer, but when he faced her, the look she gave him spoke louder than her words or his gut. "I think we need a little play time. We'll join you in a bit." Dusting off his hands, he stole a quick peck on the lips on the way by, then made the turn down the hall that led to the den and their brood.

Catching on, Holly's features mellowed. "What's going on?"

Candy forced a smile, indicating the ring of chairs around the table. The ones that had been a part of so many heavy conversations. "I think we should sit."

Her nose crinkled, their nurse didn't like the sound of that. "And why do I need to sit?" she spat as she plunked onto the hard surface.

Taking the seat next to her mother at the opposite end, Candy chewed her lip. She had prepared a small speech on the way over but couldn't remember a word of it. "Sometimes what you ask for," she began, then cleared her throat.

Her eyes wide, Holly waited. "Yes?"

"We wanted to help a young woman," Candy tried again.

Holly nodded. "That's what we do."

"Well, we have one who needs a great deal of help." Candy swallowed. "Only she isn't an unwed mother."

"Then what is she?" Holly's fingers rested on the table before her, and she lifted them, slowly curling them into a fist.

Candy grinned at the motion. "Relax, she isn't in that kind of trouble, either." Inhaling deeply, she plunged. "Michelle is transitioning. She wants to be a woman."

Holly's jaw dropped, her lips searching for words

before she pressed them tightly together. Inhaling through her nose, her nostrils flared in small spasms. "Carol and I are lesbians. That doesn't mean…" Her voice trailed away.

"I know," Candy commiserated. Taking the spoon from her mother, she mashed at a few bits of potato, then offered them to her. With Holly's strawberry-red hair, she ran hot, so her cool response had Candice on edge.

"Why would you bring some guy home to our halfway house for women?" Holly exploded.

"It wasn't my first choice," Candy explained calmly. "In fact, it wasn't my second, either. But as Glenda pointed out, that doesn't mean it won't work."

"So, what am I supposed to do?" Holly sniffed, air catching in her throat. "I wanted to—" she gasped loudly. "What about Melody? Our doctor is an obstetrician, not a plastic surgeon!"

Candy redirected the attack, understanding her disappointment all too well. "I know you were looking forward to the baby part. As much as any of us were." She cut her eyes over at her employee and friend, then returned to her mother. "There you go. Want some broth?"

"Yes, please," Lanelle slurred. She was tough, and although her time could be up any day now, if her doctor's prediction had been correct, it didn't show.

"This isn't fair, Candy," Holly stammered. Pressing trembling fingers to her lips, she felt cheated.

"I know. It's not really what we asked for, but it's who we got. A young woman who is in a great deal of pain." She could hear Holly choking back sobs and avoided looking at her. "I don't know where this will take us, but I trust fate. I have to, after so many years."

Holly dabbed at her eyes, then pushed her chair back to retrieve her coat. "We'll be over early tomorrow." She closed the door firmly, alerting those in the den to her departure.

As soon as she had gone, Candy called down the hall, "All clear. Anyone hungry?"

"We're starved!" Gary teased, appearing almost as soon as she had spoken. "Get your seats and I'll serve the bowls," he advised their children.

Daks took the end Holly had vacated, while Lane climbed into the chair opposite his Meme, who smiled at him. Her nose in the air, Joylana hoisted herself up into a seat against the wall next to her and announced, "Girls' side."

"Would you like to hear about our new client?" Candice asked when they had been served and Gary had joined them.

"I better not," he declined, having heard enough from down the hall. "I'm good for renovations, but I don't want to get involved in the client side of your little project." If he had any misgivings about the direction their endeavor had taken, he knew better than to openly share them. His wife was right about one thing; fate had a way of working things out. "I trust she's in good hands and that's enough for me."

"Smart man," Lanelle praised. Her bowl empty, she turned to her granddaughter and pointed at Gerald, Daks and Lane. "Boys' side."

"Mhm." Joy grinned, leaning into the hug Lanelle offered.

Watching them, Candy toyed with her bowl of stew and contemplated what might be going on across the street.

FOUR

All In

Holly took her time crossing the street to let the cool air sooth her raw nerves. At the wide glass door, she paused to see they had started without her. Pushing it open, then sliding it closed, she didn't bother with a fake smile. "Sorry. I wasn't quite ready to leave."

"Is everything ok?" Carol asked with genuine concern.

"Oh, it will be fine." Now she smiled, enveloped by the gentleness of her mate. "Is my plate in the oven?"

"Yes, I'll get it." Caroline jumped up, indicating the table and bottle of wine. "Help yourself, love."

Holly nodded, taking an empty seat and pouring her glass. "You must be Michelle," she offered civilly.

"Yeah," their new client quietly agreed. Pushing her half-eaten pork chop around with her fork, she groaned. "I'm sorry, I'm not up for all the pleasantries."

Holly blinked at her. "It's been a hard few days, I take it."

"Something like that." She toyed with her meal. "I'm not very hungry."

Placing her lover's serving before her, Carol advised, "I

can put that in the fridge if you like. You can help yourself to it later tonight if you feel inclined."

Michelle's mahogany orbs shifted to her friendly features, searching the clear blue eyes for clues. As if she couldn't gauge their sincerity, she shrugged. "Thanks." Leaving the table, she climbed the stairs and disappeared.

Watching her go, Holly swirled her glass, then took a large swig. "What do you think?"

Carol sat and pulled her chair up to the table. "I think we are in for a great deal of work, and getting the house ready was the easy part."

"You and I could tell Candy he can't stay," Holly hissed, her eyes still on the stairs. "If we stand together, we out rank her. Besides, it's our house."

"But that's her job. We're a team, remember? She recruits for us," Caroline quietly pointed out, not eager to take sides.

"Right. She's supposed to find girls for us. Women who need a hand. Not some man—"

"Don't!" Carol snapped, cutting her off. "I don't want to fight with you about this, especially not here in the kitchen where she might hear us!"

Holly leaned back in her chair, her plate untouched. Taking another thoughtful swallow of her beverage, she sighed. "That's it then. We're all in on this, whatever this is."

"Look, I knew you were going to be upset." Carol adjusted herself to be taller in her seat, then flicked her eyes over at Holly. "I know you, baby. You get these ideas of how things should be, and then you have a really hard time changing them to meet reality."

"You mean like getting this house? Or our wedding? Please." Holly sneered, then pouted. "I just thought for once things would turn out the way we had hoped they would."

"Oh, honey!" Carol scooted and pulled her wife into a hug. "All those things have turned out great! And you're forgetting, we've had some wonderful things, too! Our jobs, our daughter! Our lives have been pretty amazing. Some women haven't had it so good, and that's why we're doing all this."

Leaning into the embrace, Holly sighed. "I know. But can you imagine how hard this is going to be? I mean, if he doesn't have anyone in his family on his side."

"We're on *her* side," Carol emphasized.

"*Her* side," Holly mocked. Her features softened, and she repeated, "Her side." The pause grew long, and she sniffed. "Can you imagine how disappointed our parents were?"

"Our parents?" Caroline coughed, releasing her lover enough to glare at her. "What have they got to do with any of this?"

"Nothing. Everything." Holly pulled away and picked up her utensils. "I never understood why they split us up when we were young. But since we got Gracie, I get it." Taking a bite, she pointed her knife at the small round face. "Parents want things for their children. They have dreams for them. Of them. Who they will become."

"Ok, and?" Carol dared to ask, not sure she wanted to go there herself.

"And we let them down. Who we are wasn't good enough for them," Holly stated bluntly while cutting a slice of her meat. "It's only a matter of time and Grace will be making her own choices. What if she isn't who we want her to be? Are we going to toss her out, just like Michelle's parents did? Like our parents did?" She ended with a choke and covered it with a cough and a swig of wine.

"I'm sorry, but I think we are much better parents than they were. We're going to love our daughter and whoever she becomes. And we are exactly who we were meant to be. If our parents have a problem with that, screw them!"

Blue flame danced behind Caroline's eyes as she cursed the lives they had left behind. Seeing it, Holly's lips twisted into a grin. "You are so hot when you're angry!"

"Then you better get ready, because the idea of her parents not being there for her has me flaming," Carol teased, leaning forward to taste her before she asked, "Can we be ok with this?"

"I'll be ok with this," Holly agreed. "Like you said, it may take me a few days to really get on board, because you know how I hate changing plans." She laughed, considering the notion. "But yeah, I get it. And it occurs to me that Candy might be right, as bad as I hate to admit it."

"About bringing her to us?" Carol stood and began cleaning their daughter's fingers and face.

"About fate. We live in a world that accepts us, but they don't really embrace us, if you get what I mean. My heart really aches for her. If her family won't be there for her, Michelle landed in a pretty good place for second best. At least we have some idea of where she's coming from."

"We're not second best," Carol chortled. "This is the place she was meant to be, and I don't give a damn what my or her parents think about it."

FIVE

Bad Enough

"Hey there, Tom." Gerald Ford greeted his closest friend as he strolled into the fire station the following morning.

"Hey, Chief. You're here early," Tom Harris teased.

"Yeah, we've got a bit of chaos going on at our place. I just needed to get out of there," his boss explained. "Let me grab some coffee and I'll come join you."

Returning to their favorite spot at the open doors a few minutes later, Gary pulled out his lawn chair and took a seat. "Man, those girls."

"What'd they do now?" Tom asked. With the Ford household, it could be anything.

"You know they've been working on the girls' place. Converting to a boarding or a halfway house, right?" Gary shook his head in disbelief.

"Yeah, you said they were fixing it up," Tom recalled.

"Well, they got a man over there. Only he wants to be a woman or something." Gary chuckled, shrugging. "After they brought him home last night, Candy was explaining it to Holly—" he stopped short at the other man's expression. "What's wrong?"

"You said they got a dude who wants to be a woman? A black guy? About five foot tall?" Tom asked incredulously, holding his hand in front of his chest to indicate his height.

"I don't know, I didn't see him. I went to the den to play with the kids. Those girls are running that circus. I helped with the renovating, but I really don't want to get tangled up in the business part. Her name is Michelle, though. I did catch that much," Gary offered. Taking a few gulps of his hot brew, he settled back into his seat to enjoy the morning sun.

"Naw, his name is Michael. Damn, I'm sorry buddy. It was bad enough when he wanted to be gay, but now it's all a mess," Tom observed.

Gary stared at him. "You know the guy?"

His friend looked around, then lowered his voice. "He's my brother-in-law. He's stayed over at our place off and on. Good kid, but a bit squirrely. He's getting near thirty, but still lives with my wife's parents."

Gary raised his chin in interest. "Oh yeah? He's not into drugs or anything, is he?" He suddenly wished he had been paying more attention the night before.

"No, not that I know of." Tom swiped the air with an open hand, as if to push the thought out of way. "But it's trouble. You know we've been married a few years now, and Michael was flaming as long as I've known him. His parents are really churchy, so they've been pushing him to 'get right with God' and all that."

Gary's gut tightened at the insinuation. "Oh yeah?"

"Oh yeah. But a few days ago, my wife found where he's been seeing a doctor. He's going on hormone therapy and all that. When she confronted him, he told her he was going to have the surgery and make it official."

"I bet their parents really didn't like that," Gary mused quietly, his mind racing.

"Nope. They changed the locks on their house that day and told him not to come around again. They are done, d-o-n-e, with his mess. It's been tearing the family apart, the life he's living, and they don't want no more of it." Tom leaned back in his chair and wiped his lips. "Honestly, I feel sorry for the boy. I mean, what was he thinking, deciding something like that?" Tom's voice cracked, his pain genuine.

Gaping at him, Gary's mouth opened, then closed, as he considered his reply. "I don't really think it's a choice, Tom." His mind turned to their nanny and nurse, who took excellent care of his family. It hurt like hell to hear his friend use such harsh language. "Listen, I need to make a phone call," he excused. Folding his chair as he stood, he leaned it against the wall before he disappeared into his office and closed the door behind him.

Across town, Michelle anxiously sat in Candy's kitchen and waited for their first meal together. Facing the back door, the living area behind her buzzed with children's voices, but she didn't bother to turn around. She'd seen kids before. However, surprise washed over her features when they joined the table to eat.

Taking the chairs along the wall, the boys resembled each other rather closely, perhaps even a little too closely as they were obviously a good number of years apart. The younger of the pair appeared to be a typical preschooler, loudly conversing with his brother, while the older one had physical difficulties with the process. Making it into his chair, he kept pace with the youngest, and confirming Michelle's suspicions that he had special needs.

Turning her attention to the other side of the table, the girl who faced them nearly knocked Michelle out of her seat. "Who might you be?" she hissed to the small black face next to her.

"I'm Joylana," the precocious youngster replied tartly.

"These are Candy and Gary's children," Carol explained, indicating each in turn. "Joy turned five on Halloween. Lane will be three at Christmas, and Daks here is a big thirteen." She smoothed his hair as she placed his plate before him. "Sit up. That's it. Show everyone how grown up you can be." Turning to her partner, she asked, "Who was that?" as Holly hung up the phone.

"It was Gary." The nurse grinned deviously. "He said he just wanted to check on us."

"Does he do that often?" Michelle asked, still getting to know everyone. Gary had left before they arrived, so she wasn't sure what to think about him yet.

"Sometimes. Gerald Ford is a bit protective of everyone in the bubble." Carol laughed. "Of the world, truth be known."

"What's a bubble?" Their new tenant glanced between them as she accepted her serving of eggs, bacon and toast.

"We're the bubble," Holly explained, twirling her finger around to indicate the group. "That's what we call ourselves after the covid quarantine days."

"Oh, snap! I remember all about that mess." Michelle emitted a loud laugh, earning a glare from Joy. "Girl, what you gonna say?" Candy had described her home as being through the looking glass, and they were in fact an eclectic gathering.

"You should use your inside voice," Joylana rebuked,

her prim demeanor a sharp contrast to her boisterous brothers on the opposite side of the table.

Michelle's jaw dropped for a moment before she snapped it shut. "You mean I should be more lady like." She sat up straighter in her chair and adjusted her spoon in her hand. "Show me, little momma."

Joy grinned, obviously happy to do so. "Grandmother says you should do it like this."

"Who is Grandmother?" Michelle asked while trying to contort her fingers into position.

Holly and Carol laughed in unison. "Oh, just you wait," Holly chirped. "That's Eveline, Gary's mother. You'll meet her as soon as she and Roger are back in town. She will definitely set you straight. She and Joy have tea together on Sunday afternoons, and she gives her lessons."

"She gives everyone lessons," Carol seconded, rolling her eyes.

Appearing haggard, Candy quietly came out of her mother's room and closed the door behind her. On the other side, the muffled hiss and pop of her oxygen machine held a steady rhythm, and she paused for a moment to listen to it before turning to the group. Her tired eyes making the loop, she felt relieved that Holly appeared at ease with their new tenant. "Any breakfast left for me?" she asked in a scratchy voice.

"I've saved you a plate," Carol offered. "And the coffee is fresh."

"Is that your momma's room?" Michelle asked once she was seated next to her sons.

"Yes. Mom's terminal," Candy briefly explained before taking a few bites. "I guess you could say that's why we hadn't placed anyone yet."

Michelle blinked at her, considering. "I'm sorry I was

so aggressive yesterday. I know you folks are just trying to do me right."

"That we are," Holly agreed. "Gary says he'll help retrieve your belongings from your parents' place when he gets home if you can wait a day or two."

"The guy on the phone?" Michelle appeared confused for a brief moment, then huffed, "Man, I don't need none of that stuff."

"Are you sure?" Candy asked in surprise. "Gary's rather good with people. I bet he could talk them out of it for you pretty easily."

"Naw, it ain't worth it. But I'd like to get me some more new clothes if anyone…" her voice trailed away. "Or I guess it can wait."

"No, we'll take you shopping," Carol countered.

"I'll do it," Candy added. "I need to get out of here for a few hours anyway. It felt good to be out even the little bit that I was yesterday."

"What about your momma?" Michelle asked timidly.

"She sleeps a good deal of the time," Candice explained between bites. Taking her time, she eventually added, "I'm glad Glenda sent you to us. I needed at least a little distraction and a bit of normal."

"But she's your momma," Michelle pushed, her eyes growing misty. "Mine don't even want me."

"Awe, honey." Caroline dropped an arm across her shoulders, pulling her into a half hug. "You've got plenty of other people who do. I know it's rough, but sometimes families aren't made by blood."

"Nope. Sometimes they're only made by love," Candy agreed.

SIX

Feel Like a Woman

Finished with breakfast, the group cleared off the table and placed their dishes in the sink. "I'll get those," Carol advised, giving her lover a pleading glance. "Can you show them where to go?"

Her mouth drawn into a thin line, Holly nodded. "I suppose that I should. There are a few places that are better than others."

"What kind of places?" Candice asked innocently as she helped herself to the last of the coffee.

"We aren't going to find what I need at the superstore," Michelle advised.

"No, I'm afraid that you won't," Holly agreed. "Let's use your iPad and set up a route for you. I know of one store that I like the best, but I've never shopped for…" Her voice trailed away.

Candy flushed, realizing how their privacy lines would soon blur, perhaps becoming lost forever. "I'll get it. And don't worry, whatever I see I swear I won't ever mention!"

"What's she talking about?" Michelle hissed as soon as the lady of the house had disappeared.

"You live in our world, so I'm sure you understand," Holly pointed out bluntly. "As I told my wife last night, most people accept us, but not nearly as many support us or really get us for that matter."

"We're ok as long as we're not in their face," Caroline quietly agreed. "That's why we can't get what you need at the superstore."

Rejoining them, Candy laid the device on the table and opened it. "I'm a little nervous. Or maybe I'm excited," she confessed. "Will they have anything Gary and I might be interested in?"

Her two employees locked eyes in an instant of shock, then laughed boisterously. "You never know!" Holly sang. "Take your credit card and an open mind."

"Great! I can't wait," Candy agreed in relief. Retrieving her mug from the counter, she took a seat at the table as Holly plugged in the first address.

"Go here first. Ask for Tina. She owns the place, but she also works with the local clubs and shows," Holly pointed out matter-of-factly. "If she can't provide what you need, these other two shops might be able to fill in the gaps."

"Thanks," Michelle blurted, snatching up the iPad. "I'll navigate while Candy drives," she suggested.

"Sounds like a plan," Candice agreed, placing her empty cup into Caroline's suds. Pulling on her coat and gloves, she grinned. "I feel like we are heading out on an adventure!"

"It'll be an adventure all right." Carol chuckled, the idea of their boss visiting their favorite shop bringing a soft pink flush to her cheeks.

Sliding up next to her at the sink, Holly whispered, "What are you thinking?"

"I'm thinking about our last purchase." Caroline giggled, and it was Holly's turn to blush. "Yeah?"

"Stop it. You're making me hot!" Holly groaned, leaning in to kiss her.

Pretending not to notice, Candy clipped, "Are we ready?"

"Yes, ma'am." Michelle snapped her a salute, her slender face damp with nervous anticipation. "I don't know if I've ever been so happy!"

Outside, the air seemed lighter, and the threat of snow had abated, at least for the time being. Pausing in the center of the yard, Michelle stretched her arms wide and looked up at the sky between the branches of their ancient trees. "It feels so nice here, Candy. Thank you for having me."

Taken by surprise, her new friend nodded, admiring the glow of her creamy brown skin. "Thank you for coming."

Contentedly, the pair climbed into the small blue Prius they had arrived in the night before. "Do you think there's enough room?" Michelle inspected the back seat doubtfully.

"We can make more than one trip if we need to, and there's space in the trunk." Candy started the car and waited.

Michelle opened their map and began the route. "I know this place," she observed, tapping the screen as they left the drive and made their first turn. "Are you sure you're ok going there?"

"I'm not squeamish," Canice advised. "Besides, this will be a logical place to start. How long before you have your surgeries?"

"A while." Michelle sighed. "The doctor warned me

about going 'under the knife' too soon." She laughed at the expression. "I started my hormones, so my body is undergoing natural changes. It may be enough to suit me, and if it is, I won't need top surgery. So, I need to wait at least six months."

"Will you be able to afford both?" Candy asked casually as she steered the car into the shop's crowded parking lot. "It could be to your advantage if it works out that way. With the pain and the expense," she added as they climbed out into the cool air.

"I've saved enough for both," her charge explained. "But I want it to be right, so I guess I'll try the little fake boobs first."

Candy grinned. "It would be nice to get to choose the size, that's for sure."

Michelle eyed her warily as they approached the glass entrance. "Are you poking fun at me?"

"Never!" Candy laughed out loud. "I'm just a little jealous. Most girls are stuck with what they get." Grasping the handle, she led the way inside, pausing to take in the view as they entered. "Wow, this place is amazing!"

Michelle had been there a few times and didn't see the big deal. Noticing the clerk, she gave her a small wave. "Hey, Brenda."

"Girl, look at you! Are you finally making the move?" The clerk sauntered onto the sales floor to give her diminutive client a half hug.

"I feel like a woman." Michelle flicked the line of her jaw with the backs of a few fingers. "My skin gets softer every day."

"Oh, those hormones will bring on the changes quick," Brenda agreed. Noticing Candy, she offered her hand. "Are you a friend of Michelle's?"

"Absolutely," Candy replied as she shook the

appendage. "Candice Ford. Michelle is staying with some friends of mine. They said we should see Tina."

"Eew, sorry, Tina is over at the club doing a fitting," Brenda advised. "She'll be back later, though, if you need her."

"I think we're ok." Michelle shrugged as she wandered between the racks. "You remember those jellies we talked about? I've decided I need to get me some."

"Oh, the enhancements. Wonderful!" Brenda clasped her hands in delight. "Let me get the case and you can look at sizes."

Leaving the pair to their measuring, Candy wandered the store, mostly interested in the collection of shoppers rather than the goods. Every age, size, sex, and race seemed to be represented, and she felt empowered with the knowledge of such a place she had never heard of before that morning.

"I have this one." A brunette woman of about Carol's height tapped on a glass case Candy had been perusing, indicating a thick shaft.

Imagining her two friends visiting the location to make such a purchase, Candy flushed. "I'm sure it's wonderful," she managed.

"It really gets my girlfriend screaming," the shopper added.

"I bet." Candice stepped back, unable to look her in the eye as she turned towards the fitting rooms. "How's the hunt going?" she called into the row of curtain-clad cubicles.

"I actually like this set," Michelle replied with glee, again proclaiming, "I really do feel like a woman!" Tossing back the screen to reveal her broad smile, she slipped out to stand before a full-length mirror next to Candy. Hardly taller than her benefactor, she bumped her with her shoulder and squared herself to the glass. Wearing a thin camisole, it hugged the bulges naturally, and she used her palms to trace the new curved form of her chest. "Too big?"

"No, they look great!" Candy beamed at the image, noticing how the change suited her. "I can see how pleased you are with them. Now we should get you a few changes of clothes, and even some accessories if you like."

"What kind of accessories?" Michelle turned and admired the side view. "Like a purse and stuff?"

"And makeup. Jewelry. Have you thought about a wig, or what you might do with your hair?" Candy asked eagerly.

Her dark eyes sliding to the side, her new friend glared at her. "You don't like my hair?"

"No, it's not that," Candy sputtered. "It's just having Joy, I know how challenging it can be."

Michelle gasped in relief, having forgotten about the youngster for a moment. "Who's her daddy, anyways?" Turning to the racks behind her, she picked up a few blouses to lay across her new assets for inspection.

"Well, I don't really know." Candy sighed, a little let down by the change in topic. But in the end, she had known it would eventually come up. "We adopted Joylana five years ago. Someone left her in the box at Gary's station when she was only a few hours old."

Stopping cold, Michelle slowly pivoted to face her. "You mean that little girl was abandoned?"

"Yes, you could say that." Candy appeared anxious. "I don't talk about it often. She's our daughter, and it hurts to think someone…" her voice trailed away, and she sniffed.

"Man, that's rough." Michelle drew her into a hug. "I'm sorry, I didn't know it was like that!"

"You thought I had a baby with a black man," Candy added for her.

"Well, I ain't met this Gary of yours. Maybe he's a black man." Michelle laughed guiltily, fully aware that their two sons attested differently.

"I know." Candy forced a smile. "And I might as well tell you that Dakota's father isn't in the picture, either. He was mine, and Lane is ours…together."

"I think they're all yours together," Michelle corrected, returning to her search. "You do have your hands full." Doing a bit of quick math, Michelle arrived at Candy's age at Dakota's birth. "Is that why the house is for unwed mothers?"

"Oh, that is a part of it, I guess," Candy agreed with a shake of her head. "But we also have Grace, who was born to one of Gary's younger cousins last year, which is what really inspired us. But in the end, we all have our reasons. All have our stories," she added quietly.

"Stories I'm now part of," Michelle lamented. Taking her selections to the back, she wanted to try them on and to have a few minutes to herself while she considered what she had learned.

Alone again with the other patrons, Candy made another loop around the store, this time coming to a few racks of lingerie. Choosing a frilly pink one, she located her size. Her fingers trembled when she lifted it from the stand.

"A man or a woman?" Brenda asked, interrupting her thoughts.

"What?" Candy had been holding the find up to her small frame, but let it drop quickly.

"Your lover. A man or a woman?" the clerk repeated.

"My husband is a man." Candy flushed, presenting her selection. "I've never really worn this sort of thing."

"Oh, darling, don't be nervous!" Brenda gushed. "It's never too late to add a little spice to the bedroom."

Candy stared at the pink lace. "There's enough spice." Her voice quavered. "I've lost some weight since we first met. I guess you could say I grew up chunky, and I never imagined wearing such a thing."

"Oh," Brenda's voice went up and down as she drew out the single syllable. "I bet you'd look amazing in it. Want to try it on?"

"No!" Candy practically screamed. Flicking her hand, she rolled the negligee into a ball and glanced around to see who might be looking.

"Is that for Gary?" Michelle asked as she joined them.

"Uh," Candy stammered, regretting ever touching it.

"It's ok. You're allowed to be sexy, Candy." Michelle teased.

"Am I?" Staring at the floor, the mother of three giggled. "I'm not so sure about that."

"Go try it on. Come." Michelle gripped her arm firmly and guided her to the back. Selecting a stall, she pushed her friend inside. "Do you need help?"

"No, I don't need any help!" Candy squeaked. Swallowing, her hazel eyes met Michelle's mahogany orbs. "I seem like a coward, don't I."

"Only if you don't try it on!" Her salacious smile beckoned Candy to join her. "Come on, girlfriend. Live a little."

Pressing her lips together, Candy nodded. "Ok, I'll try it." Of course, that meant she would have to show it, which terrified her.

Stepping out, Michelle slid the curtain into place. "Don't worry. I won't judge."

"No, but I might," Candy grumbled to herself. Pulling

off her clothing, she took her time, removing each piece more slowly than the one before it. Working the lace into place, she frowned at her reflection. "Michelle?" No reply. "Brenda?" She poked her head out, locating the two at the end of the row. "I'm not coming out there."

Joining her, Michelle pulled the curtain and scooched up beside her. Looking her up and down in the mirror, her smile slowly faded.

"What's wrong?" Candy demanded, having nothing to do but stand there, practically naked.

"Nothing." Michelle shook her head, then dabbed at a tear. Swallowing, she managed, "I want to look like this." Her fingers unsteady, she reached out and trailed the lacy cup that lined Candy's creamy white cleavage.

Shock freezing her in place, Candy's chest heaved. Sensing her fright, Michelle whispered, "I used to keep magazines of girls dressed like this hidden under my bed. My momma found them once. She thought I was a typical boy, lusting after those girls." She laughed anxiously, her finger still toying with the lace. "She had no idea what was in my little mind. It wasn't lust. It was hard wishing. I'm so jealous of you."

Candy swallowed, her eyes flicking up and down her short frame reflecting back at her. "It's hard to imagine being envious of this," she teased.

"Oh, I definitely envy you. I wanted to be those little girls in their skimpy little outfits. So badly it hurt." She withdrew the hand and laid an arm across Candy's shoulders so they squared side by side before the mirror. "I'm almost there, though."

Candy stared at the pair of them. "You really think I look ok in this?"

"Girl, I think Gary is going to pass clean out when he

sees you, and I don't even know the man!" Michelle pulled her arm out of the way and turned to leave.

"You don't know him yet," Candy corrected, smiling at her curves and turning for a better view. However, she had a sneaking suspicion she could be right.

SEVEN

On a Scale

What Candy had imagined as a short shopping spree turned into a full day extravaganza. They had finished with the clothing just as Tina returned to the shop. Overjoyed with her new look, the owner had insisted on gifting her a wig in celebration.

After another full hour of searching, Michelle had made her selections, purchasing two others to complete the package. "I need options!" she teased as they stacked the boxes in the back of the car.

"And you need a manicure!" Candy cajoled, pointing at the spa down the street.

"No!" Michelle squealed, obviously overjoyed at the idea. "Can we?"

"I wouldn't dare take you home without it." It felt good to see the girl she had thought of as surly blossom, and Candy grinned broadly as they moved the car closer to the salon, then made their way inside.

Taking seats side by side, each made their selections for acrylic nails and polish. Candy chose a sensible length coated in soft pink that would complement her new negligee. Smiling, she secretly couldn't wait to show her purchase to Gary and hoped he would be as thrilled with it as she was.

Michelle on the other hand went all out. Her new nails half an inch long, she had each tipped with bright red that accentuated her new feminine curves and long maroon waves.

"I think we should have a facial while our nails dry," Candy observed. "I'll call the girls and see if we have time, since we are having guests this evening."

"Oh! I don't want to impose," Michelle rebuked. "Really, you've given me so much already."

"Honestly, it's no bother," Candy insisted, ready to dial. "They're friends and family. They'll understand."

Stepping outside to hear without the chatter of the salon, Candy let Carol know how their day had progressed, and that they would be home a little later. Then she returned to her charge with a loud, satiated sigh. "All set. See, I told you it would be easy."

"Do you pamper yourself like this all the time?" Michelle asked as she reclined in her chair and blinked at the lights above her.

"Not at all." Candy giggled. "I couldn't tell you the last time I had a spa day. Maybe I need one more often, to be honest."

"I can't believe it," Michelle breathed as they climbed back into the car. Admiring her nails, she gasped. "My boss won't even recognize me!"

"That's the idea, isn't it?" Candy observed. "This is a whole new you!" Pausing, her nose crinkled. "I guess I didn't realize you still had a job."

"Oh, yeah. I must not have explained. I took a few days off after everything blew up at home, but I should be going back to work in a day or two. I need to look at my schedule." Tossing her bright red curls over her shoulder, Michelle opened her new bag and fished out her phone. "How do you keep them from smudging?" she asked, inspecting the tips of her fingers.

"You don't dig around in your purse," Candy teased as she pulled out onto the road. "I guess we're ready to go home?"

Next to her, Michelle glared at her phone. "Actually, I need to go by the store if that's ok."

"Which store?" Candy covered her break peddle, preparing to change their destination.

"Carter's Furniture on Main Street. I asked for a few days off, but I'm not on the schedule for next week either. I need to find out why," she groaned. "Dammit. I wasn't ready to quit yet."

"Oh." Candy's lips puckered, considering the situation. "Do they know you're in the process of transitioning?"

"Yeah. I had to tell them something," Michelle explained, tucking the device back into her purse. "Janice didn't say there was a problem with it." Flipping down the visor, she inspected her makeup. "My lashes feel all clumpy."

"Don't pick at them," Candy advised. "You'll need to wash the mascara if you want to remove it."

"It kind of itches," Michelle lamented. "I want to try the falsies next time." She opened her tube of lipstick to reapply the creamy shade. "Thank you for doing this. I can't believe how different I feel."

"You look great," Candy agreed as they parked in front of the furniture store. "Listen, when we get in here, we need to show a firm hand. They can't just fire you for no reason. Or for this reason," she added angrily.

"Yeah. Or can they," Michelle replied quietly.

Walking briskly, the pair entered through the wide glass doors. Not hesitating, Michelle led the way to the counter near the back, where the Carters stood gaping at her approach.

"Why am I not on the schedule?" Michelle demanded without preamble, her loud voice strained. "At the busiest time of the year, you better have a damn good reason to cut my hours."

"We've been slow," Mr. Carter excused. Looking her up and down, he did a poor job of hiding his shock at her changed appearance.

Her eyes roved over the showroom, spying at least a dozen heads floating among the sofas and love seats. "Fool. I see all these people in here. Don't give me 'slow' like I ain't got eyes."

Intervening, Candy huffed, "You know it's illegal to fire someone for their gender and or sexual orientation," confident transgender qualified.

"He isn't fired," Janice Carter clarified. "We reduced his hours, that's all."

"None isn't reduced," Candy quipped, having seen and heard enough. "*For Women* has an attorney in house. I was hoping we wouldn't have to use him." Grabbing Michelle's arm to pivot her, she practically dragged her away from the sales desk.

"*For Women*? Is that the name of our house?" her client hissed. Trying to keep up, she fought for balance in her new heels.

"No," Candy growled back, continuing to lead. "I don't think we really have a name."

"Do we really have a lawyer?" Michelle pushed as they approached the door.

Before Candice could explain, Mrs. Carter caught up to them. "Please, girls. Let's talk."

Stopping short of the glass exit, Candy snapped, "Unless it involves giving her hours back, I think we should go."

Janice breathed in deeply, then groaned. "You have to understand. Michael is one of Calvin's favorite salesmen. He loves the guy."

Michelle's features twisted, her lip taking on a quiver. Seeing her distress, a wave of fear washed over Candy at what she might say next. "He has a funny way of showing it," she snapped.

"Yes, well, he's disappointed, that's all. You have to understand. Men are all part of a club. A fraternity of sorts. He feels like Michael has turned his back on their order, and that's one thing Calvin will never accept," the older woman explained.

"So where does that leave me?" Michelle sniffed, fighting actual tears. "I've been here for years. You can't just toss me out. I helped build this store, dammit!"

"I know, hon," Janice commiserated. "And I know it's not much, but I can offer a severance package. Or maybe call it a gift, if you will. Once you've had your surgeries, you can come back. Maybe Calvin will have a change of heart by then."

Seeing the months of limbo looming ahead of them, Candy's voice cracked. "That won't do!" Standing at full height, she fumed, "You can't just put her on hold and money won't make it right."

Michelle held up a hand, her new nails sparkling at the tips of her extended fingers. "How much money? On a scale, how much is my leaving quietly worth to you?"

Candice gasped. "You can't be serious!"

Michelle's lips curled into a bitter sneer. "Well?"

"I can write a check for ten thousand right now. You can cash it at the bank just a few blocks over," Jan advised.

Candy tossed up her hands and turned her back. Sidling over to the window, she watched the cars through the glass while the other two women haggled behind her. A few minutes later, she noticed the silence and looked around, but the pair had disappeared. "Well, I guess they hit a good number," she deduced with a sigh.

EIGHT

One Step
_____

That night, Candy checked on her children, who played together in the den, before joining the rest of the group gathered in the dining room. They rarely used the formal space, but tonight they needed the room to accommodate their numbers. That, and it meant putting a buffer between them and her mother's suite.

"Everyone's going to get along this evening, right?" she asked, only half listening as she mentally counted chairs and tidied the room. "There's Ben and Melody. I don't think Matt is coming, and Gary is out, but we'll have Bella, Annette, Carol, Holly, and add Michelle. Oh, and Gracie. But she can hang off a corner. Yes. We should have enough chairs."

"I want to sit with the big people," Joylana whined, pulling her mother away from her planning.

"Oh, honey, but you already ate, remember? You and Meme had dinner almost an hour ago." Candy squatted before her and looked into her mahogany orbs. "You can sit with us next time. Play with your brothers tonight, ok?"

Joy's lips formed a small pout as she looked over the

collection of firetrucks, houses and cars her siblings busily arranged for their favorite game. Candy sighed, aware that her daughter's interests had transitioned away from such things over the last year. "Just for tonight, sweetheart."

Selecting a seat on the couch, Joylana climbed onto it and inspected her doll's hair. "She needs a brush," she announced curtly.

"That's the spirit." Candy handed her a small case of accessories. "Maybe Santa will bring you another baby this year."

"With dresses," Joy advised, drawn to her task.

"Yes, with dresses," Candy agreed. Standing, she pointed at her sons. "You boys play nice!"

"Yes, ma'am," they mumbled in unison, hardly distracted from their building.

Leaving the den and making the turn, she discovered their attorney and family friend Benjamin Monroe had claimed the head of the enormous table. His girlfriend, Dr. Melody Castleberry, sat next to him facing the door. "Oh, you're the first ones here. That's good! It'll give us a chance to talk before everyone else arrives."

"Yes, we do need a good chat," Melody eagerly agreed, glancing at the man beside her.

"How is Lanelle doing?" he asked in a somber tone.

"About the same." Candy took a seat at the far end and managed a weak smile for Holly, who entered carrying a highchair for Grace. "I don't wake up fearing today is the day anymore, so that's good news."

Ben stared at her, dumbstruck. "That's, uh, ominous sounding," he stammered.

Holly shook her head. "No, she isn't being morbid or anything. I just shared a bit of my wisdom. Lanelle's body is going through a process, and there are certain milestones that let you know the end as near."

Candy nodded, pouring herself a glass of wine. "If mom is still making it to the bathroom and coming out of her room every day, I know we still have a bit of time left."

"Oh." Ben chuckled. "That actually makes a lot of sense."

"Yes, it does," Mel agreed, covering the top of her glass as Candy offered to share. "I'm going to pass on the wine tonight. Do we have any tea?"

"Sure. I'll get it," Holly agreed. Her face contorted at the odd request, she glanced between the couple as she left to help with the remainder of the meal.

"Is Gary not joining us?" Ben asked. Filling his goblet from Candy's bottle, he chortled, "I took his chair, but it's only funny if he shows up to see it."

"No." Candy laughed with him. "He's on second shift, so he won't be home for a couple of days. But, if it works out the way he planned, he'll have four days off across Christmas this year."

"Man, I don't see how he keeps those hours," Ben lamented, then stood as three more women, one of them carrying Grace, joined them. "Ladies. Looking lovely this evening," he observed, then jokingly added, "I'm surrounded by estrogen! Hello Annette! Bella, my sweet!" He leaned in to give her a hug, then offered the third a small wave. "I'm sorry, I don't believe we've met. Are you a friend of Bell's?"

The air felt hot for a moment as Michelle looked quickly around the room. Her eyes resting on Candy, she remembered to breathe. "No, I'm a guest of Carol and Holly's" she explained lamely.

Also getting to her feet, Candy coughed in surprise, then indicated the couple with an open palm. "Ben, Melody. This is Michelle." She smiled broadly as she introduced their newest member.

"Hello," Melody approved with a small nod. "I didn't realize anyone had moved in yet." Her eyes darting to her host, she raised her brow in an unspoken question.

"She arrived yesterday," Candice explained as she pointed everyone to seats. "Bella, take the one you want and just put Gracie next to you. Or maybe I should let you have this end." "Oh!" Michelle moaned, making the connection. "You're Grace's…" her voice trailed away. "I'm sorry. I didn't realize I would be meeting you tonight."

"Nor I you," Bella spat, looking her up and down as she tried to put the toddler in her chair.

"Bell, don't be rude," Annette commanded.

"I'm not!" Bella denied. Giving up on the seat, she lifted Grace into her arms and cast a confused glare at the adults surrounding her. "I thought the halfway house was for pregnant girls."

A unanimous exhale escaped the group just as Carol appeared at the door with the serving tray. "Everyone have a seat, this thing is heavy!"

Hearing the urgency in her voice, they quickly rearranged and got everyone into a chair and the food into the center of the table before anyone else spoke.

Smoothing her new skirt over her lap, Michelle inhaled deeply a few times. Turning to Bella, who had landed beside her, with Grace on the end, she smiled. "I'm so sorry. Candy and I spent the day together and she has told me so much about you. About all of you!" She cast her eyes anxiously around the gathering.

"Yes, I did!" Candy blurted from the seat she had managed to retain at the end. "Only, I didn't really have a chance to tell everyone about you," she added more quietly.

A cool silence settled over them, and Michelle whispered, "I see. Well, meeting is just one step, and there are many more to come."

"Are you a man?" Bella squealed.

"Bella!" her mother snapped.

"I've never met a tranny before," the teenager pushed. "Does it hurt?" she squarely addressed the elephant in the room.

"No, baby, it doesn't hurt," Michelle replied gently. Shaking her head, she tossed back her new burgundy locks and laughed. And not a small laugh. A full-on belly shaker.

"What's so funny?" Holly muttered, confused by the display.

Righting herself, Michelle lifted her glass and held her grin. "I have had an amazing day. My new bestie took me out for the greatest spa day I ever could have imagined." She raised a toast to Candy, then took a noisy sip.

"I'm glad you enjoyed it," Candy said meekly, mortified by her young cousin's behavior.

"I truly did." Turning back to Bella, Michelle toned down her smile. "Now. I thought from my conversation with Joylana this morning that this was a house of manners. So now I ask you. Do I look like a man?"

Bella swallowed, seeing clearly the error of her ways. "I'm sorry. That was quite rude of me."

"Yes, it was." Michelle nodded her agreement. "But I forgive you, seeings how we just met. My name is Michelle Miller. No, I'm not a pregnant girl. I am in the process of transitioning, so you can refer to me as she or her."

Candy's chest swelled with pride, and she turned to the one her new comrade had just put in her place. "Well, what do you say?"

Bella's eyes filled with tears. "I'm sorry, Auntie. I didn't mean to offend your friend." She swiped at the drops of sadness. "I'm sorry, Michelle. I was angry. I shouldn't have done that to you."

Seeing her sincerity, Michelle came to her rescue, pulling her into a hug. "That's ok, darling. I really have heard wonderful things about you."

"Did you hear what a mess my life is?" Bella sniffed loudly, fighting to hold her voice even.

"Honey, what's happened?" Annette asked, her face covered in bewilderment. "You haven't said anything about any of this."

"I was trying to be brave. All grown up, you know?" The girl flushed. "And now I'm so embarrassed." She looked around, noting that she was flanked on all sides by people. Unable to escape, she sighed. "Let's serve the plates, and I'll tell you about it."

Michelle nodded, happy to give her center stage. Following routine, each platter and bowl was passed, and the plates served before they began to eat.

Once they were ready, Bella took a deep breath and plunged. "Billy has a new girlfriend. One of the girls at his college," she announced in a shaky voice.

"And Billy is?" Michelle prodded.

"Grace's birth father." Bella sat up straight to look her in the eye. "I thought somehow, some way, we were going to be together at the end. But we aren't." Her lips trembled, but she held back the tears.

The group around her shifted anxiously in their chairs. "Teenage drama," Ben articulated. "Bell, honey, boys are just dumb, ok? You can't let him upset you so much."

Candy coughed. "I wouldn't call them dumb. They just make mistakes, like we all do." She gave their young cousin a supportive smile. "We all know how you feel, having loved and lost. It's painful, but it's not the end of the world," she promised.

Holly and Carol shared a glance, giving each other a nod. Seeing the motion, Bella groaned. "I'm being silly. I know it." Pushing her anguish aside, she leaned towards Michelle. "Tell us about your day."

Shaking her head slowly, the newcomer sighed. "Like I said, it was an amazing day. Right up to the point I got fired."

"Wait, you got fired?" Ben gasped, obviously stricken. "Candy wanted us to discuss something." He tapped the table with a stiff digit and glared at her across the length of it. "Was this it?"

"Yes." Candy frowned at her plate. "Her boss is a jerk. It was tense, and I might have mentioned we had an attorney," she tried to explain. "I'm sorry, Ben."

"Well, you do have one, more or less." He shook his head in disbelief, then continued his interrogation. "Who's your employer?"

"Carter's down on Main, but just relax, ok?" Michelle waved a palm in a circle towards him. "I already got it all handled."

"Did they actually say you were fired?" Benjamin pushed, his lawyer instincts in high gear. "I mean, obviously you might want to build a case, and that will be a pivotal point."

Michelle reached inside her blouse and pulled out the check Janice had written. "Does this not say fired?"

Ben accepted the rectangle of paper, emitting a low whistle. "That's quite a sum. Is it good?"

"We don't know," Candy lamented. "The lobby was closed at their bank by the time we got there, and the drive through wouldn't cash it. Now we have to wait until Monday before we can be sure."

"Well, once we know, I'll have a better idea of what we should do next. This was her idea, though, right?" He gave the check a small wave, then handed it back to its owner.

"She offered me ten," Michelle explained, returning it to her bosom. "I wasn't having that, so we discussed it and come up with that."

"Hmm." Benjamin appeared thoughtful. "It could be considered extortion, depending on the context. But then again, it does look like a bribe from another angle. What I can tell you is, if it doesn't cash, I'll put the paperwork together for a lawsuit if you want."

"Hell yeah, I want," Michelle squealed. "I put my blood, sweat and tears into that store right beside them since I was twenty. And besides that, leaving was not my idea! I totally deserve that money if they are going to push me out like this."

"I agree, you should be compensated, especially if they are letting you go because of your decision to transition. That's a protected criterion. Like it or not, discrimination doesn't fly," their attorney pointed out somberly.

NINE

Not That Simple

"Gosh, I feel exhausted," Holly complained the following morning as she helped Lanelle into her favorite chair at the table for breakfast.

"It's a good thing it's Saturday," Candy agreed as she distributed the plates.

At the far end, Michelle sat twisted in her seat so she could watch the children playing on the other side of the wide door. "Are they always this well behaved?"

The women laughed, and Candy explained, "Joylana is playing wowoos with them, so it's peaceful. If she decides to do something else, it won't go so well."

"It's tough when they can't let you be who you are," Michelle lamented. Turning around, she opened the camera on her phone and used it as a mirror so she could adjust her hair.

"That looks nice on you," Lanelle complimented.

"Yeah, I like it. But the red was more fun." Michelle closed the device and smiled. "This is my rest day wig."

"What about the other one?" Carol asked as she placed pancakes onto the plates. "Didn't you get three?"

"Yeah." Michelle sighed. "The other one will be my 'get a new job' wig I guess." She waved her hands around her head. "It's kind of a bun thing. I thought it would give me a professional look at the store."

Candy observed the droop that settled over her new friend's body. Stepping over, she dropped her arm across her shoulders and squeezed. "You know, it could be your 'going to classes' do. They have tons of interior design degrees at the colleges here."

"Oh, I don't know about that." Michelle smacked her lips as she pulled herself free. "School might have been all right for you folks, but I never enjoyed it." She looked at the other women one at a time. "You're all way smarter than me with your college educations." She stopped when she came to Lanelle. "How about you? Did you go to college?"

"No, I missed out on that," Lanelle rasped. Using her fork, she managed to cut a square of her flakey breakfast. "I need syrup," she observed.

"I don't think women were encouraged to get degrees back when mom was young," Candy pointed out gently. Taking a seat on the back side next to her, she poured the sweet coating for her.

"Well, it ain't that simple," Michelle insisted. "First, I'm staying with you nice people." She indicated the girls while fixing her own serving. "And I'm kinda in the middle of something." She wafted a hand to indicate her new physique.

"I think this is the perfect time to set some goals," Caroline pointed out before leaving the discussion to wrangle the kids.

"And you are welcome at *For Women* for as long as you need us," Holly quietly agreed. She grinned for a moment, happy with the name Candy had bestowed on their endeavor.

Michelle froze, her fork suspended inches from her mouth. "I thought you didn't want me around." She glared at the nurse accusingly.

"I never exactly said that," Holly denied. Taking the end seat also next to Lanelle, she mused, "I have to admit, I wasn't expecting you. I really think there are some girls out there who might need us." She anxiously adjusted a napkin across her lap, then reached for Lanelle's plate to give her a hand.

"So, you're making an exception for me," Michelle deduced.

"Something like that," Holly agreed, not looking at her.

Feeling the tension rising, Candy desperately wanted to avoid another scene anywhere close to the night before. "Why don't you think about it? There's lots of time to decide, and classes start every semester, so this spring or next fall makes little difference in the end."

"Yeah, I'll think on it," Michelle halfheartedly agreed.

Joining them, the boys took the outside seats, facing the wall, while Joylana claimed the one between Michelle and her mother. "Hello," she greeted her cordially. "You have new hair."

Michelle grinned at her. "Good morning, little momma. I do have new hair." She used a free hand to strike a pose to exaggerate it. "How you like?"

"It's very pretty." She mimicked the move, highlighting the short puffs that adorned each side of her head. "How do you like mine?"

Michelle ran her tongue over her teeth as she considered Candy's words. "You're cute as a button," she commended.

Joy beamed at the praise and eagerly cut into her short stack. However, she had someone new to converse with, and made the most of the prospect. "Do you take tea?"

"I love tea." Michelle sat up straighter in her chair. Her mannerisms normally quite exaggerated, she did her best to reign them in. "Will you be having tea with Grand-mother soon?"

"She's out of town," Joylana explained. "We haven't had tea in weeks." Shaking her puffs side to side, she conveyed her sadness at the thought of it. Catching a whiff of excitement she added, "We could have tea tomorrow, couldn't we?"

"Oh, I don't know, baby. Grandmother might be upset if we had tea without her," Michelle quickly pointed out. She searched the faces of her hosts to gauge their response. "Let's wait until she's back from her vacation, and then we can talk about me joining you." Michelle noted the glance that passed between Holly and Carol and snapped, "What. You don't think she would have me over for tea?"

"With Eveline, that's hard to say," Holly confessed.

"Eve can be quite opinionated," Candy quickly explained. "In fact, she and I haven't always been on the best of terms."

"Pfft," Carol spewed. "That woman. You say this and she does that."

"I like her," Lanelle chirped. "She's a good friend."

Silently looking one to another, none of them could argue with that.

Across town, Gary poured his morning cup of brew. Through the glass wall of the conference and break room, he could see Tom waiting for him at the front door. "Damn," he muttered. It was obvious he would have to go out, but their last conversation put a rock in his gut.

Pouring a second cup, he sauntered outside and handed it to his friend. "Good morning."

Tom looked up at him, his features contorted from deep thought. Accepting the offering, he muttered, "This ain't my mug."

"It'll wash." Gary chuckled, pulling chair out to have a seat.

"You talked to them girls?" Tom asked gruffly.

"Yes, I've spoken to them a few times." He waited, forcing his friend to commit to the conversation.

"How's he doing over there?" Bingo.

"*She* is doing quite well," his boss stipulated firmly. Watching, waiting, he sipped his brew.

"Jesus," Tom muttered, shaking his head. "You know, it ain't smart to side against your wife on family matters. Especially when it's her family."

Gary's features softened. "I know. And I'm sure this puts you in a tight spot. But you said you had a good relationship, so why does that have to end?"

Tom turned slowly in his seat to face him. "He ain't one of the guys anymore," he pointed out bitterly. "Why would I want a relationship with *her*?"

"That's for you to decide, my friend." Gary took another long, purposeful sip before he continued. "But it's been my experience that people are who they are. They don't change for us. They change for themselves. Michelle was inside that guy you liked, and that guy is still inside of her. There's no reason you can't sill care about her, or at the least like her a little bit."

Tom's mouth fell open, but his angry rant didn't come.

Snapping it shut, he glared at his boss as he measured his words. "I'll have to think on that," he finally said more quietly.

Gary raised his cup in a mock toast. "Glad to hear it," he simply replied.

TEN

In Between

"Daddy!" Lane squealed as Gary came through the back door. Catching him around the knee, he squeezed his father's leg affectionately.

Hoisting him up, Gary laughed. "Hello, little man!" Giving him a poke in the chest, he asked, "What have you been up to?"

Lane simply pointed at the front room, where an extensive village had been constructed. "Wowoos, daddy."

Picking up one of the cars, Grace made it onto her pudgy legs and waddled towards them. Waving it around, she seconded, "Wowoos."

"Well, I believe that's her first word," he chortled.

"She says momma, too," Carol countered from her position at the sink. "We just had breakfast, would you like some?"

"No, we were in and ate at the station before I left." He inched his way over to the doorway where he could get the full view of the scene. Michelle sat at the far end of the sofa with Joylana perched next to her. Spread on the ottoman lay her complete collection of dolls and accessories. "Oh boy," he muttered.

Hearing the muffled voice, Michelle looked up and smiled. "Hello! You must be the infamous Gary."

"And you must be the notorious Michelle," he teased.

Her expression shifted to surprise. Her eyes and mouth all open in shock, she gasped. "Notorious! What did I do?"

"Nothing." He shook his head as he pulled off his coat and dropped it over the kitchen chair before crossing the room. Taking Lanelle's comfy seat, he indicated their collection. "It's nice to see Joy with her dolls for once."

"She's a girly girl," Michelle pointed out smugly. "Just like me."

Gary nodded. "That red hair really suits you." He swallowed visibly, preparing to get all the bad news out of the way as quickly as possible.

"Thanks. Your wife helped me pick it out." She had been brushing a doll's shiny locks and held it towards Joy for inspection. "What you think, little momma?"

"It needs a braid," Joylana suggested.

Gary snickered. "She'll have you at that all day if you let her."

"It's ok. I don't mind it." She glanced up at him, sensing his tenseness. "Relax, bubba. This is your place. I'm just visiting here."

"I know." Gary ran has hand roughly around the back of his neck and squeezed. "And I've been looking forward to meeting you. I'm sorry I left too early on Friday to do it then."

Michelle paused her motion and rested the doll on her lap. Concern clouded her features. "Is something wrong?" She was good with vibes, and his vibe wasn't good. When he remained silent, she looked at the girl next to her. "Hey, little momma. Would you go see if Carol will pour me a glass of that tea she makes?"

"Sure." Joy carefully laid her baby to sleep while she was gone.

"Ok, what's going on?" Michelle hissed. "I know you got something to tell me."

"I do," Gary confessed, feeling caught between a rock and hard place. "And sooner is better than later." He smiled at her, hoping he appeared friendly. "Your brother-in-law is at my station," he announced calmly.

"My—" she splayed her hand against her chest as she gasped. "My brother-in-law is at your station. Tom. You know Tom," she stammered.

"I know Tom," he confirmed quietly as his daughter returned to present her prize to Michelle.

"Why thank you, momma." Taking the glass, Michelle took a hearty swig.

"Would you like a glass, daddy?"

"Oh yes, please, princess," he confirmed with a pat on her back. Alone again, he gazed at their guest. "I just thought you should know."

Michelle ran the back of her arm across her lips to dry them. "Thank you for telling me. I wasn't sure how he was going to take all this. Everyone else done washed their hands with it," she explained.

"That's what he said. But he also said you two were friends. I'm hoping you still will be once everything settles." Gary smiled, accepting his glass. "Thank you, sweetheart. I'm going to sit back here in Meme's chair and watch you play. Would that be ok?"

"Of course, it is, daddy." Joylana beamed, not noticing the tears that Michelle struggled to hide.

Leaning back against the cushion Gary soon fell asleep.

Noticing his quiet snore, Michelle laughed. "Does he always do that?" she asked as Candy joined them.

"Yes, unfortunately." Candice sighed. "His first day home, he'll be tired and maybe a little grumpy. But after that, we'll get three good days. The kids still have school tomorrow, but they get out early on Wednesday."

Michelle noticed the gloom in her features. "You don't like his schedule," she observed.

"That's no secret. I've struggled with his choice of career, but I've learned to live with it," Candy explained. Joylana had joined the boys and Grace with the wowoos, so she started packing up the dolls. "We all make sacrifices for those we care about," she finally admitted.

Helping with the cleanup, Michelle nodded. "I know that's right. Speaking of which," she began, but the doorbell rang, effectively cutting her off and jolting Gary awake with a "huh?"

"I'll get it," Carol called, making it to the portal first. Swinging the massive door wide, she gasped, "Bella! Why on earth are you ringing the bell? You should have come to the back like family," she rebuked as she let her inside and closed the wooden panel behind her.

Grinning sheepishly, the teenager presented the large arrangement of flowers she'd been holding. "These are for Michelle."

"For me?" She blinked rapidly, standing to accept them. "I think your whole family just wants to see me cry," she accused playfully. Turning the vase to inspect them, she shook her head. "They are lovely, Bella. Thank you."

"They're 'I'm sorry' flowers," the girl explained. Slipping off her coat, she sniffed. "I really hope you can forgive me."

"Hush now." Michelle wafted a hand at her. "That's all water under the bridge. Candy, where should we sit these?"

"How about the kitchen table?" The lady of the house pointed. "Put them right in the center."

Fighting his way to his feet, Gary glanced at his half empty glass of tea. "I think I need some coffee. Anyone else care for a cup?" he offered.

"Make plenty," Candy suggested as the group migrated to the stiff wooden chairs. Peeking into her mother's room, she shook her head at her mother's wide-awake gaze. "Are you nosey or hungry?"

"Just nosey," Lanelle rasped. Pushing at her covers, she added, "Help me to my chair?"

Candy grinned, never tired of that chore. "You know I will," she whispered with Holly's advice in the back of her mind. Once she was settled, Candy helped herself to the coffee and took her seat next to her on the back side, between her mother and her mate.

Sitting opposite Lanelle, Bella beamed. "Ok, now I can tell you why I'm really here." She rubbed her hands together anxiously.

"Oh, so my flowers were like an afterthought?" Michelle accused, giving her a playful punch.

"No." Bella laughed. "They were the ice breaker. But I do have something I need to get your advice on, now that my head is a little clearer," she began.

"Let's hear it then," Holly commanded. Making a cup for herself, she joined them, taking her usual end seat next to Lanelle.

"You know, we should call this the round table," Caroline observed from the far end. "We have so many good discussions seated here."

"Hear hear." Gary toasted then gulped, aware he wasn't normally part of them.

Bella curled her lips, then sighed. "I've decided since

Billy isn't really waiting for me at that fancy school of his, I'm not going to go."

"What?" Four voices cried out once.

"No, no!" Bella waved them off with her hands and laughed. "I mean, I'm not going to his uppity college. And, I'm not going to med school." She looked at Holly apologetically. "I looked online, and I want to stay here. I know it's not the degree my mother wants me to get, but I'm really thinking about interior design."

"Really?" Michelle gasped. "Did you guys put her up to this?"

Taken aback, Holly gaped at her. "No, we didn't put her up to this! Why would we?"

"But you know what they say, great minds think alike!" Carol pointed out diplomatically.

"Why?" Bella asked in confusion. "I never told anyone I was interested in decor."

"Not you." Candy raised her chin at Michelle. "We were just telling her yesterday that she should go to school here. She's also interested in design."

Michelle shook her head slowly while pulling her arms across her chest. "I didn't say I would go," she pointed out succinctly.

"Oh my gosh!" Bella squirmed in her seat. "If you start in the fall, we could go together."

Michelle appeared perturbed. Tapping her mug with her long red tips, she took in each face one by one.

"You can't argue with fate," Candy pushed. "Sometimes when things start falling into place you just have to go with it."

"But I'm not really sure that's what I want," Michelle whined. Turning a palm to the ceiling, she lamented, "The next thing you'll be talking about opening a shop together."

"Shut. Up!" Bella squealed. "That would be amazing!"

"Wow," Holly coughed. "I don't think I've seen you this excited about anything in a while. Are you feeling ok?" Her forehead crinkled, she studied the girl's features anxiously.

"Yeah, I'm great!" Bella practically shouted. "I just suddenly realized what I want to do. What I *really* want to do. Doesn't have anything to do with Billy. Isn't that great?"

Michelle smiled knowingly. "So, you're really not here to talk me into something?"

"No." Bella panted. "Should I be?" She looked around with a confused expression. "Am I missing something here?"

"No, you're not missing anything. And I'm glad you're finding your way. That's what life's about, after all. We all just need to find our way," Michelle reassured as she offered her new friend a hug.

ELEVEN

The Last Minute

"Three, two, one," Gary counted as he held back the curtain that covered the window next to the front door. Outside, he had a great view of the end of his driveway.

"What are you doing?" Candy asked from her seat on the opposite end of the sofa.

"Watching the kids get on the bus. And go!" He leapt into action, grabbing his jacket and shoving his arms into the sleeves.

"Where are you off to?" Michelle asked while maneuvering around him with her cup of coffee. Taking the opposite end of the couch, she tipped it towards Candy. "Girl, your man is crazy."

"They'll be home early," Gary hurriedly explained. "I still have some shopping to do, and this is my last chance since I go back in tomorrow."

"Oh," Michelle made the connection. "You waited to the last minute. Typical man." She smacked her lips and took a sip of her hot drink.

Still scrambling, Gary gave Candy a peck on the cheek and headed for the back door. "You girls have a good day," he called over his shoulder as he closed the exit behind him.

"He is polite, though," Michelle added, peeking out the window he had vacated to watch him go.

From the kitchen, Lanelle craned her neck to see as well. "Are you ready to get up?" Holly asked, noticing the action.

"Yes," Lanelle croaked, accepting her help to stand. But on her feet, she surprised her nurse by shuffling towards the living room.

"Honey, where are you going?" Holly snapped. "Your oxygen doesn't reach in there."

"I need more line," Lanelle urged, pushing for her favorite comfy chair.

"Wow, Mom!" Candy grinned up at her. "Are you joining the girls today?" She stood and helped her mother into her recliner as Holly adjusted the cord.

"There, I think that's enough," the nurse observed as they helped her charge lean back in the seat. "Is that comfortable?" she asked doubtfully.

"Yes, much." Lanelle sighed. "Thank you."

"Ok, well I guess we are making camp in the living room today." Holly held up her hands in mock surprise. At her feet, Gracie and Lane played with a few cars. "Ok guys, Meme is resting in here today, so you have a new boundary."

"Why?" Lane whined, eager to climb under his grandmother's raised feet.

"Because we need some room around Meme's chair," Holly insisted as she scraped away the toys that were inside her comfort zone. "Carol, do you have a broom handy?"

Michelle watched the commotion with wide eyes. "What's she gonna do with a broom?" she murmured.

"Nothing serious, I don't think," Candy replied, equally entranced.

"Hush, you two," Holly spat. Accepting the device, she placed it across the middle of the floor, then tossed the remaining toys to the other side. "You play over there. This half of the room is for the grownup," she explained.

With a slight pout, Lane pulled at Grace's arm to move her. "Let's go, Gracie," he instructed.

Michelle grinned behind her cup. "You have such wonderful babies," she observed.

"They're precious," Lanelle agreed. Lying back against the cushion, she adjusted the blanket Holly had draped over her, then pulled her arms across her chest. Breathing deeply, she sighed.

The room quiet, they all watched her hands move up and down as her air moved in and out. "How peaceful," Carol observed as she took the other chair.

Still pacing the room, Holly appeared a bit lost. "I like her room better. But I guess this will do." She perched on the ottoman and chuckled. "So, I guess we get a bit of round table talk without the table. Anyone got anything new?" She smiled, hoping to pass for relaxed at the unusual behavior of her patient.

"I can't sit here long," Caroline advised. "I need to get the bedrooms in shape before their holiday starts."

"Oh, hush," Michelle pawed at her. "You can sit with us for a few minutes." She glanced around deviously. "I wonder what Gary rushed out to buy."

Candy flushed. "I'm sure he's thought of a gift," she offered meekly.

Spying the pink hue, Michelle giggled. "Does that mean he got his present early?"

"What present?" Holly asked, noticing the color change as well.

"Candy bought him a little something special at the shop the other day," Michelle hinted.

"That was a secret!" Candy gasped, startled at being exposed.

The two women laughed, and Holly coaxed. "Oh, Candice. We wondered if you found anything you liked at our favorite shop. Tell us. What did you get?" She turned on the ottoman so that she could place her hands on her employer's knees. "Don't be shy."

Candy's heart raced. "Well, I did see something you might have liked," she shot back. "It was about this long!" She held up a finger on each hand to demonstrate the length of the shaft she had seen inside a glass case. "Another patron was telling me all about it."

Holly's turn to blush, she fumed, "Stop it!" But it was too late. She cut her eyes over at Caroline, who burst into giggles.

"Do you mind?" Lanelle rasped. "I'm dying over here. With all this racket I can't even concentrate." She squinted to see their reaction, then laughed herself. "You thought I was asleep, didn't you."

Their peals even louder, Michelle held her side. Pointing at Candy, she squealed. "But she even had her nails painted to match hers!"

Carol's jaw dropped. "Candy, what did you buy?"

"It was a negligee. And yes, Gary really liked it," she proudly confessed, giving Michelle the evil eye. "You weren't supposed to tell."

"But that's what girlfriends do, isn't it? Share each other's secrets?" Her eyes wide, her expression morphed into something more. Something almost desperate.

Noticing the change, Candy gasped. On her knees, she crossed the cushion between them and pulled Michelle into a hug. "Stop it. You know you're among friends. You don't need to test the limits here."

Clinging to her, Michelle sobbed. "I don't know what's wrong with me. I swear I've cried more here than I have in my entire life."

"It's the hormones," Holly quietly observed. "They will level out as you adjust."

Candy hugged her firmly, rocking her back and forth. "Shsh," she hushed. "Cry if you need to. We've got you, girlfriend."

An odd silence enveloped the room, and the girls respected the quiet, so everyone jumped when a voice called from the kitchen, "Knock knock!"

"Oh my God," Candy scolded the woman standing in the doorway. "Melody! You scared the bejesus out of us!"

"Sorry, I really did knock, but since there was no reply, I let myself in." She smiled brightly, hoping they weren't too upset with her.

"Here," Caroline offered while getting to her feet. "You can have my seat. I have bedrooms to attend to."

Accepting, Melody pulled off her coat and draped it over the arm, then sank down on the cushion.

Staring at her, Holly's eyes narrowed, but she didn't mention her suspicions. Instead, she offered, "Baby, can you get Mel a glass of tea before you head upstairs?"

"Sure," their nanny agreed. Smiling when she presented it to her a moment later, she observed, "I guess you've closed your office for the holiday?"

"Closed, yes," Dr. Castleberry agreed. "I run on a three-day week now. Mondays, Tuesdays and Thursdays. After the b—" she froze. Giggling, she tried again. "Soon I'm going to cut those hours as well. I'm thinking eight to one three days a week should be enough to keep the bills paid and still give me time for…other things."

"You're pregnant," Holly blurted, then snapped her fingers. "I knew it! The other night when you asked for tea. You never drink tea!" she squealed, leaping to her feet to hug her.

"Seriously?" Candy blinked at her, watching the display. "Don't you know what causes that?" she asked in dismay.

"Yes, I'm quite aware." Melody laughed, pushing herself up to accept the squeeze, and then another as Caroline joined her.

"You don't look very happy about it," Michelle whispered to the girl frozen on the couch.

"Candy has a bit of fear where pregnancy is concerned," Melody pointed out as she adjusted back into her seat. "I can't blame her for that. I have my own trepidations, but what's done is done." She rubbed the smallest of pooches at her midsection and grinned.

"I didn't realize you were even trying," Candy observed, her words monotonous, as if she were in a trance.

"Were you trying?" Carol took the ottoman, no longer caring about the cleaning.

"Not exactly. But that's the thing about having sex," Melody pointed out bluntly. "These things tend to happen, intensions or not."

"What about Ben?" Holly's features crinkled with concern. "The man's almost fifty."

Melody coughed a loud laugh. "He's forty-four, but yes, he was pleasantly surprised. At forty, I'm the one taking the most risk." She rubbed her bump again, licking her lips. "I never realized how badly I would want this until it happened," she explained quietly.

"I squashed your news," Michelle lamented. "The other night, you were going to tell everyone then."

"It's ok." Melody smiled at her. "It was nice to welcome you to the group, and I had other chances to share."

Michelle stood on shaky legs. Reaching her, she leaned across, giving her a firm squeeze where she sat. "This is such a safe place," she whispered.

"It is," Melody agreed. "They saved me, just as they are saving you. One day, when I'm ready, I'll tell you all about it," she promised.

TWELVE

Be a Rebel

"Does that mean I won't see you for a few days?" Michelle quipped as Gary donned his coat on Thursday morning.

"That it does," he agreed, giving her a nod. "You know the fireman's life. Two days on, four days off, and there we go."

"That's the best shift," she agreed, glancing around to see that they were alone. "First shift changes too quick, and third drags it out too long."

"Agreed." Gary grinned at her. "I'm glad you're here, Michelle."

"Me too." She returned the smile, then inhaled deeply. "I was wondering," she added, hesitating for another peek. "Could you give someone a message for me?"

"Sure, I could," he readily agreed. "What do you want to tell him?"

"Just tell him I'm sorry. I never meant to hurt him. And I really do miss being his friend. If he ever wants to come over for a game or something, I'm down." She looked at the floor, anxious about what her brother-in-law would reply.

"I'll let him know." Gary nodded, turning to the exit. "I'll see everyone in a couple of days," he called before he closed the door.

"Him, huh," Carol teased from the other side of the wall. "I didn't realize you had a boyfriend."

"Damn it," Michelle muttered, not realizing they'd been overheard. Stepping around into the kitchen, she winced. "You know how it works, right? Gender and sexual orientation aren't the same thing?"

"Oh." Caroline gasped. "I'm sorry. I didn't realize you were a lesbian."

"Who's a lesbian?" Candy asked, joining them from her mother's room.

"I'm not a lesbian," Michelle groaned, throwing up her hands. Taking a cup from the cabinet, she poured it half full, then selected her seat at the table to wait.

"I guess it's time to talk," Holly observed as she closed Lanelle's door.

"Yeah," Michelle replied in a surly tone, indicating the other chairs. "You guys make me do this every day."

"Think of it as therapy," Candy advised. Selecting her own mug and filling it, she joined her. "But start at the beginning, because I missed it."

"We were talking about the difference between sexuality and gender." Caroline caught her up while she also chose a chair. "And I think Michelle has a boyfriend, but I'm a little hazy on that part."

"I do not have a boyfriend," Michelle insisted, then slumped in her seat. "Not yet anyways." She glanced between their eager faces. "You really want to hear this, don't you."

"I'm all ears," Candy informed her, then took a sip of brew. "After you outed my negligee, it's your turn to share something juicy."

"Oh, come on," Holly groaned. "A nightie isn't juicy."

"Hey, I said that he liked it. What more do you want?" Candy laughed.

"Guys, let her talk. I for one want to hear this," Carol shushed them.

"It's not that exciting," Michelle advised. "I was just explaining that gender, which is feeling like a woman or a man, isn't the same thing as sexuality."

"Sexuality is who you are attracted to," Holly provided.

"Exactly," Michelle agreed. "Back when I was first coming out, I was too scared to tell people that I was a woman. So, for a time, I just told everyone I was gay."

"Why would you do that?" Candy crinkled her nose at her.

"It was easier." Michelle exhaled loudly. "I like men, ok?" She grinned deviously at Candice. "I have to tell you, Gary is hot, girlfriend."

Candy's cheeks flared, and she choked on her swig. "Gees, you don't have to say it."

Holly giggled, but her wife also flushed, avoiding her gaze. Noticing, she nudged her. "It's ok. That was a long time ago."

"I know, but sometimes it creeps up on me," Carol lamented.

"What?" Michelle asked. "Come on, more secrets! Damn, you guys are incorrigible!"

"That one's a little painful," Candy confessed. "But Holly's right. It was a long time ago."

Michelle's smile faded as she read the hurt in Candy's demeanor. "I guess I'll leave that one alone then. Instead, I'll just tell you, that's really the step that got me where I am today. Being gay. It didn't take me long to know for sure. I wasn't a man dating another man. I wanted to be his woman. I wanted things this body I was born with could never fulfill." She opened her hands in disgust. "I knew I had to move forward," she finished gruffly.

"You only have a few months to go," Candy pointed out hopefully.

"Or less," Michelle corrected. "I've been thinking I should go ahead with the bottoms. I can still wait on the tops to see how well my boobs come in."

"You can get the two separately?" Carol asked in surprise. "How does that work, exactly?"

"They just take all my boy junk and turn it into girl junk. Down there." Michelle shrugged. "And I can wear the fake knockers as long as I need to."

"It's not really that simple," Holly clarified. Reaching across the table, she gripped Michelle's hand. "But know this. I'm a nurse, first and foremost. When you decide the time is right, I'll be there for you with whatever care you need."

Michelle's bottom lip quivered, but she smiled. "Thanks. All of you, really. You girls have no idea how much this means to me."

"Good morning!" Gary called as he approached the station. "We've got company," he observed, as a few of the others had joined their morning ritual.

"You guys are always hanging out here, we thought we'd give it a try," Bruce explained.

Seated in the chair next to him, his buddy Jim seconded, "Yeah. Can't let you guys have all the fun."

"Suit yourself," Gary teased. Shuffling past them, he made his way inside and searched for his mug.

Under the pretense of another serving, Tom joined him. "I guess we won't get to talk much today."

"Or you could be a rebel and put it all out there in the open," Gary countered, taking a large swallow of the hot liquid.

"Naw, I'm more for keeping things on the down low, thanks." Tom laughed, filling his cup. "How's she doing, though?"

"She's good, Tom. She said she'd be ready to watch a game with you any time." Gary slapped him on the arm and smiled. Having said what he needed to say, he headed to his office and passed on the sunshine for that day.

THIRTEEN

Boy Meets Girl

Gary's two days at work passed quickly. Raring to go at quitting time on Saturday, he sauntered out to his suburban, but paused short of his trusty ride at the sound of heavy footfalls crunching the snow behind him. Spinning around, he gasped. "Hey, Tom! I thought you already left."

"I did," his friend confessed, shifting his weight anxiously. "But if I go home, I'll just sit there and wonder. And then I can't leave, you see?"

Gary stared at him. "No, I guess I don't see." His brow furrowed, he groaned. "Try again."

"I need to follow you home," Tom explained. "That's the only way I'll get to talk to Michael. Err, Michelle. Without my wife knowing."

Gary pursed his lips, considering their options. "You're not going to say or do anything, you know. That would upset her. Are you, Tom?"

"What do you mean?" The other man shrugged.

"Well, that first day we talked about her, you said some things. Let's just say they were, uh, inconsiderate." Gary nodded, waiting for a response. Getting none, he stated more bluntly, "I can't let you hurt her, Tom."

"I'm not going to hurt her. Dammit, I thought you wanted me to be friends with her. You said so." Tom stomped his cold feet, confused. "Can I go see her or not?"

Gary grinned, slapping him on the shoulder. "Sure. So long as we understand each other. Michelle's one of my girls now, that's all."

Tom's features twisted as he considered the notion. "Whatever you say, boss man. I'll follow you." Turning on his heel, he made his way over to his step-side pickup and climbed in.

Making the turn out of the parking lot, Gary watched the red vehicle close behind him. Flicking open his phone, he made a quick call. "Hello. Holly? Yeah, I'm on my way. But I'm bringing a surprise for Michelle. No, she doesn't know, so just tell her I'm coming from the station. If she wants the surprise, I'll be there shortly. If she's not ready, tell her to go upstairs and stay there."

Not waiting for the reply, Gary ended the call and shoved the device into his pocket. Behind him, the red chevy hung close and they pulled into his driveway a minute later. Stalling as they climbed out, he wanted to be sure Michelle had time to hide, if that's what she wanted.

However, he found her sitting at the table as they entered the back door. "Oh. You're here."

"Where else would she be?" Tom asked in a gravelly tone.

"Hi, Tom," Michelle greeted, getting to her feet.

Gary glanced between them, then around the empty room. "I guess everyone is giving you some space."

"Yes. I told them it was ok. That we needed to talk," Michelle explained.

"Ok." Gary held up his hands. "I'm going to be right in there." He pointed into the living area. "If you need anything, just yell," he instructed as he stomped his way past her.

"Jesus," Tom muttered, shaking his head. "You'd think I was an axe murderer, or something."

Michelle giggled. "It's ok. I get it, now. They first told me he was protective of everyone in the bubble. I guess I'm official." She raised her hands in a mock cheer. "Yay!"

Tom looked her up and down. "Where'd you get the tits?" he asked bluntly.

"Oh, Tom." She laughed. "They're called enhancements. I like to call them jellies. They're basically fake boobs that sit in your bra."

"Ah." He raised his chin, indicating clarity. "They look nice. You look nice." He used a hand to indicate her complete form.

"Does that mean you approve?" she asked in the faintest of voices.

"No. I can't say that I do." He shook his head. "But then again, I'm just the out-law. It's not up to me."

She nodded. "I understand. I was hoping that you would, too." She held her arms wide so he could get a better look. "I'm the me I was always meant to be. This is my safe place. This is my haven," she concluded, using her hands to indicate the full length of her body.

Tom wiped his face to remove his perspiration. "You look amazing. I don't know what I was expecting, but I can see this really suits you. Is that what you wanted to hear?"

"It sounds better," she agreed with a grin. "Do you mean it?"

"Yeah." He nodded vigorously. "I don't know that it does us much good, though." He turned, as if to leave.

"That's it? You just came to look?" Her voice quavered.

"I'll talk to your sister," he promised, his back still to her. "I'll see if I can't persuade her to come for a visit. It might do her good to know you're ok." He opened the door and left before she could reply.

FOURTEEN

The Me You See

On Sunday morning, Michelle stood before her mirror in her bedroom. Her makeup had taken a while, but with each day of practice she got better at the application. The dress she chose fit perfectly, and she produced a small grin as her palms traced the outline of her emerging figure.

Noticing Holly in the doorway, her smile faded. "Does this work for afternoon tea?"

"You bet it does." Holly leaned against the frame and sighed. "You've come a long way, hon."

"I have?" Michelle's face lit up, and she showed her full set of teeth. "I guess it's ok that I'm here?"

Holly stiffened, and she forced a chuckle. "I guess it was obvious I had my doubts."

"Yeah, you wanted a pregnant girl." Michelle rolled her eyes, turning from her looking glass to face her. She sighed, folding her hands in front of herself to toy with her fingers.

"Don't be nervous," Holly commanded. "Eve isn't as bad as she sounds. And she means well."

"Yeah," Michelle sputtered, staring at the ceiling above her. "I'm beginning to see why Glenda chose this place for me."

"Why is that?" Holly straightened herself and sauntered into the room. A pair of upholstered chairs flanked the large window on the far wall, and she selected one. Taking her seat, she waited for her new friend to join her.

Accepting the other cushion, Michelle licked her lips, sucking them in as she formulated the words. "You really are good people. And I'm ok here. No one is pushing me or making demands on me, and I can just…be. No one ever really knew me in my old life. I was all fake, and not the me you see now." She coughed a short laugh and pointed at her chest. "These fake boobs are the most real I've ever been."

Holly grinned, the girl's enthusiasm lifting her spirits. "I know what you mean. Sometimes I don't feel like my life was real until I moved here and married Caroline. And now we have Gracie!" She shook her head, as if to clear it. "It's so hard to believe I'm not dreaming."

"I'm glad you let me be a part of it," Michelle whispered. Tears tickled her lashes, and she used a fingertip to catch them before they could drip. "Damn. There goes the mascara."

Holly stood and stepped into the private bath. Pulling a few squares of tissue from the roll, she presented them with a flourish. "You're not a real woman if your mascara never runs."

"Jesus." Michelle accepted the offer and applied it to the droplets. "You girls have taught me so much. I can't believe I've only been here a few weeks."

"Come on." Holly cocked her head, indicating the door. "I'll walk you over."

"Thanks." On her feet, Michelle followed her down the stairs, where they donned their coats for the trip over. "I'm so glad it finally snowed!"

"Yes, we do love our white Christmas," Holly agreed. Sliding the back door, she warned, "Watch the steps. They tend to get a little slick."

Holding the rail as instructed, Michelle took care, then quickened her pace to catch up. "Did Candy warn her? About me?"

"She told her about you, yes." Holly chuckled, thinking of Bella and her outburst. "There's no telling what these Fords might say if you don't."

Michelle laughed, hoping it was a joke. When she caught Holly's glance, she toned it down. "You're serious."

"Just," Holly raked the air with her hands, "go easy, ok? Eveline is the head of the family. And a bit pushy. If you get on her good side, you're in."

"You make it sound like the mob or something," Michelle teased as they reached the back stairs.

"It practically is," Holly replied with a straight face. "I'll wish you luck now, before we go in," she added as she opened the back door and stepped inside.

Stomping their feet, the pair dusted off the snow, then removed their jackets. The room empty, Michelle paused to listen. "I think they're in the front room."

"Yes, we are," a loud, unfamiliar voice replied from the other side of the wall.

"That's Eve," Holly mouthed, pointing in the direction of the call.

Michelle nodded, giving her a thumbs up. Hanging her coat on the rack behind the door, she breathed deeply, then smoothed her dress.

Going first, Holly crossed through the doorway into the living area. From Lanelle's chair, Eveline watched her come, then cocked her head to follow Michelle's tentative steps.

"There she is," the matriarch observed.

"There she is," Joylana echoed, grinning big enough every tooth showed.

"Hey, little momma," Michelle replied. The sight of her small friend calmed her nerves, and she waved. "Are we having our tea today?"

"Yeah!" Joy squealed. Leaping off the couch, she darted past her and mounted the stairs. "Come, Grandmother!" She used one hand for the banister, and the other to urge her on.

Rising slowly, Eve paused next to their guest. "My granddaughter speaks very highly of you."

"Does she?" Michelle gasped for air. "She tells me good things about you, too."

Eve bowed her head slightly and raised an open hand. "After you."

Breathing out in a loud huff, Michelle turned and followed the tiny clicks ahead of her. "Very nice shoes," she praised when they reached the top. Pausing, she inspected Joy from head to toe. "And what a lovely dress."

"We are quite formal for tea," Grandmother explained, also stopping at the top before indicating the door to Joylana's room. "Everything is prepared," she assured.

Stepping inside, Michelle felt as if she were slipping in time. Back through the years, to her own bedroom. The little girl's room she never had. "I remember this place," she whispered.

"You had a room like this?" Eve asked in surprise.

"Oh, no." Michelle smiled weakly, shaking her head. "I dreamed of it though." She nodded. "I'm happy to see that Joy has such a space for herself."

"She needs it," Eveline agreed. "Shall we sit?"

"Yes." Joylana took her hand, pulling Eve towards a small chair, one of four at an equally tiny table. Once her grandmother had been placed, she returned for Michelle. "You get this one," she instructed.

Michelle sat, wondering for a moment if Joy were in fact the head of the family.

FIFTEEN

Love and Tea

With the two women in place, Joylana checked her pot and then poured three cups. Each sitting on a saucer, she carefully added a frosted pastry on the side and presented them. Michelle watched the precision in her serving and smiled. "She's so elegant. I admire her confidence."

Eveline nodded. "I've waited many years for a young lady to raise."

"Yeah, I heard that Gary was your only child." Michelle grinned. "But he's a good man. You did a good job there, too."

Eve studied her, then accepted her share. "Thank you, my love." She dipped her chin slightly to her host and smiled approvingly. Taking a bite of her cookie, she made a show of enjoying it.

Following her example, Michelle nipped a corner, then sipped her tea. "Wow, this really is delicious," she praised, not at all exaggerating. Catching Eve's watchful glare, she nodded. "My fingers aren't right, are they."

"No." Eveline cut her eyes over, then laughed. "Here, let me show you."

After a few minutes of direction, Michelle tried again. Joy held up her cup as well for comparison. "She almost has it, doesn't she Grandmother?"

"Almost," Eveline agreed, taking another sip. "Don't worry, she only needs a little patience and practice."

"The two Ps." Michelle giggled. "The two things everyone could use more of." She paused, directing her cup towards their empty chair. "I see we have room for one more."

"That chair is for Grace," Joylana explained. "Grandmother says she can join us when she is three."

Michelle nodded. "You're planning ahead."

"Always." Eveline sipped. "I heard you've done a bit of planning ahead," she shifted the topic smoothly. "In your preparations for your new life."

Michelle gasped, unsure what to say. "Little pictures have big ears," she warned.

"Yes, they do," Eve agreed. "Keep it simple." Placing her teacup on her saucer, she turned to Joy. "Do you need more, precious?"

"No, ma'am," Joylana replied crisply, taking an interest in her cookie. "I believe the icing is perfect today."

"Do you always talk in front of her?" Michelle asked doubtfully. "It can't be good for her to hear too much grownup conversation."

"It's perfectly good for her," Eve countered. "I wish to acquaint her. To prepare her for the ways of the world. My Joy is a sponge, absorbing what she needs to become a strong woman. She's a Ford." Eveline's eyes narrowed as she studied their guest. "As you may be a Ford as well."

Michelle coughed a laugh. "I'm no Ford. I'm barely a Miller." She paused, exhaling a long sigh, feeling overwhelmed. "I don't really know what I am. I mean, I know in my heart that I'm a woman. But where this woman belongs is hard to say. This is the first place I've been that ever felt like home."

"As I suspected, it was foolish of those girls to think they could have someone come and go so easily," Eve growled from behind her cup.

"What does that mean? I'll be stuck here and won't ever leave?" Michelle's eyes brimmed with fear.

"Oh, I'm sure you will leave when the time comes. When you are healed and sufficiently ready. At least most of you will. But part of you will always be here with us." Shaking her head, Eveline clicked her tongue. "You poor dear. Perhaps you aren't a Ford yet. But you could be."

"What does that mean, exactly?" Michelle squinted at her, trying to riddle it out.

"To be a Ford?" Eveline huffed noisily. "It's a state of mind. A preparedness to face life and take on challenges." She held up a closed fist, as if shaking it at an unseen enemy. "Turning ten into fifty. Now that's a Ford!" Eve thundered.

"Oh." Michelle gasped. "Someone told you."

Eveline shrugged. "Only that you were handed a pile of lemons, but you skipped the lemonade. You, my dear, went straight for the meringue pie. The last step will be spending it wisely." She toasted her with her tiny cup of tea.

Michelle coughed. "You're saying I've got balls. Surely you see the irony in that."

"Don't be silly." Eveline chortled. "I'm a Ford. I have a set of my own. And these are the kind not so easily removed."

Michelle cackled, and Joylana joined her, then appeared stricken. "That's not very lady like," she rebuked.

"I know." Michelle ratcheted down her voice. "But I'm learning. Will you teach me, little momma?"

"Oh yes," the youngster nodded vigorously. "And now every week I will have two loves with my tea. Grandmother and Michelle."

At that moment, a shadow appeared at the door, then stepped inside. "I'm sorry," Holly stammered. "I hate to interrupt, but Michelle has a visitor downstairs. I'm afraid it can't wait."

Blinking at her, Michelle's chest tightened. There were only so many people who knew her location, and none she would expect to arrive uninvited.

SIXTEEN

Room Enough

Taking the steps one by one, Michelle gripped the banner tightly. Breathing deeply in and out, she prepared herself to face whoever waited for her downstairs. Part of her hoped that it was her mother. That she had somehow found her. Had come to her at last, supporting her on her journey.

But in the back of her mind, she knew who she would find. Turning at the bottom, she stepped through the wide opening and faced her. "Mariah," she whispered.

Her eyes wide, the woman at the table gaped at her. "Oh. My. God." She slapped her hands flat against the surface before her. Behind her stood her husband. His sullen expression said it all.

Tom raised his chin. "Good morning," he called to her. Glancing at the counter, he motioned lamely. "They made us coffee. So we can talk."

"Screw the coffee," Mariah snapped, glancing at him over her shoulder. "And quit lurking. Sit down, you giant fool."

Michelle winced. Her hands drawn into fists, her mind

raced. *Be a Ford,* she breathed. *Strong, and ready to face anything.*

Pivoting, she opened a cabinet to select a few mugs. "Here Tom. Have a cup with me." She poured the brew defiantly. Cutting her eyes over at her older sibling, she dared her to object.

Tom accepted the warm beverage, then pulled out a chair next to his wife. "Thank you," he muttered.

Placing hers at the opposite end, "You want some?" Michelle clipped.

Mariah's lips parted, the air escaping through them slowly. "You look so different."

"I told you," Tom grunted. "She's a totally new person." He extended a flattened palm towards her as evidence.

"Not totally," Michelle soothed, easing her chair from beneath the table. "But enough," she added, sinking down onto the flat surface. Taking a slow, deliberate drink, she waited.

Mariah pressed her lips together firmly. Her eyes narrowed, she didn't give in to her brother's invisible game of chicken.

After the pause grew long, Michelle laughed. "I thought you'd be angry. I guess you got it under control." She toasted her sister with her coffee, then finished it off.

Her jaw tightened and Mariah spat, "I'm beyond angry. I'm livid."

Michelle chuckled again, feeling her strength swell within her. "Ok. Then why did you come here?"

"I had to see it for myself. If I passed you on the street, I wouldn't even know you," Mariah huffed.

"You've never known me," Michelle gave her a cheeky reply. "This is the real me," she added quietly. She didn't need to fight. She needn't shout have her say. "I'll ask again. Why did you come here?"

Mariah's eyes softened. She had never seen this flat calm before. "Why would you do this to us?" Her bottom lip quivered. "To me?"

"This isn't about you." Michelle shook her head slowly. Her red ringlets moved against her breasts, and she smiled. Catching one of them, she tugged it gently. "Michael is gone, Mariah. I use the name Michelle now."

"You will always be Michael Haven Miller to me," Mariah challenged through gritted teeth.

The air caught in her lungs, and she recalled her conversation with Tom the day before. "Haven. Yes." She indicated her full body. "This is my haven. The real me." She smiled deviously. "All right, I'll be Haven."

Mariah flopped back against her chair, as if she'd been punched. Her jaw dropped, she searched for the right words. The ones that would convey how ludicrous that would be.

Haven held up a stiff digit. "Nuh-uh. You said I could be Haven. And you'll be ok with that. Otherwise, why else are you here?" She opened her hands to the ceiling, her face contorted with the question her sister had yet to answer.

"Oh my God," Mariah spewed, bordering on a laugh. "He's in there. The same stubborn. Annoying. Guy." She indicated the woman across the table from her. "Is in there."

Haven smiled broadly. "Yeah, I am."

Hot tears spilled over onto Mariah's cheeks. Turning to her husband, he held her as her shoulders shook. "Oh my God," she repeated, then muttered it again.

Standing, Haven's heels clicked as she rounded the table.

Stopping behind her sister, she placed gentle fingers on her shoulder and squeezed. "You don't want to let Michael go. And I get it. What I really need to hear, big sister, is if there's room enough in your life and in your heart for me."

Extricating herself from Tom's embrace, Mariah stood. Her vision lost to a curtain of tears, her fingers fumbled, searching for her sibling. Finding her shoulders, she pulled her into a hug and squeezed. "You can still be my Haven. I can do that," she sobbed.

Holding her with her left arm, Haven held out the right, searching for her brother-in-law. Seeing the effort, he caught her hand and pressed their palms together firmly. "Thank you," she whispered when their eyes met before pulling it away. Wrapping Mariah with it, she rocked the sister she had lost, but with his help was hers once again.

SEVENTEEN

Let's Be Jolly

A fresh blanket of snow coated the street when Haven threw back her curtains to look outside. "Oh, wow," she breathed. With childlike glee, she pulled on the jeans she had purchased and turned to inspect them in her mirror.

Talking to her reflection, she rebuked, "I know you love the dresses, but there's a time to be sensible." She indicated the wonderland outside and added, "And this is it."

Applying her makeup in record time, she grinned at the result. "Perfect." Topping it off with a soft red sweater, she searched for her new boots and snatched them from the box. "Thank God Candy talked me into these!"

She smiled fondly as she thought of her petite friend. The one who had told Glenda that Michelle wasn't what they were looking for. "We see how that worked out." She beamed at herself one last time, then waved as she exited the room.

Downstairs, the girls had opened a few gifts with Grace and now waited for her. Together, they would trudge over to the Ford residence for the full celebration.

"Are you ready? They're waiting on us," Holly informed her while shoving packages into a bag.

"Oh, I can't!" Haven bounced in place. "Tom is coming to pick me up for a bit, but I'll be back before lunch. I have a nephew to meet!" She threw her arms in the air and sang, "Let's be jolly, everyone!"

"Oh, hon, that's wonderful." Tears filled her eyes as Carol pulled her into an embrace. "I'm so happy for you."

Squeezing her back, Haven blinked a few times, then surrendered to her droplets of joy. When she had been freed, she selected a tissue off the table and dabbed at them. "Proof. I'm a real woman." She held up the smudges as evidence.

"Yes, you are," Holly agreed, showing her full set of teeth. "I'm so proud of you. Go enjoy your family, and we'll save a place for you at the table."

***

Hours later, Haven entered the Ford house via the back door. Finding the kitchen empty, she quickly removed her coat and hung it on the crowded hooks before joining the group scattered about the living room. "Oh, did I miss dinner?"

"No, we've been sharing our annual toasts," Gary explained, offering her a glass of wine. "It's kind of a tradition."

"Thank you." Haven gingerly accepted it, then shuffled closer to the door.

Seated on the ottoman, Eveline raised her goblet. "It's your turn, dear."

"Oh, I don't know what to say!" Haven smiled, wiping a sweaty palm against her denim.

Standing next to her, Roger dropped an arm across her

shoulders. "Just share what's in your heart," he suggested, giving her a quick squeeze before dropping the appendage.

Casting her eyes around, Haven noticed Lanelle reclined in her place, along with Melody seated in the second chair. "Hello," she greeted her with a small nod. Along the sofa sat Candy, Carol and Holly, while Ben and Gary enjoyed the space in front of the fire.

"My heart is so full," she stammered. "I don't really know where to begin. So, I guess I should thank you. Would that be good enough?" she asked doubtfully.

Candy sighed. "If that's what you need to say, then it's definitely enough." Standing, she pulled her new friend against her and squeezed.

Her breathing under control, Haven giggled. "I guess I could make an announcement." Holding on to Candy, she pulled her around so that they faced the group together. "As most of you know, I'm going to be Haven. My sister agreed, and we can do that."

"What a wonderful name," Melody toasted, sloshing her tea slightly as she caressed her growing bump.

"Yeah. I really like it," Haven crooned. "And, I'm also ready to set a date to start my surgeries, so I hope you will all be there to support me with that. I think you will." She licked her lips, nearing the end. "And I've decided I'm going to donate the money. What Carters paid me. I'm giving it to *For Women*."

"Oh my gosh!" Carol covered her mouth with trembling fingers. "But honey, that money was for you."

"I know." Haven shrugged. "But I have more than enough, see. And I never would have gotten it without the strength you all gave me." She swallowed. "I've been lucky. And I want you to have it so you can give all those pregnant girls what they need."

The silence that settled over the group profound,

Haven looked around, meeting one gaze at the time. "What'd I say?"

Holly cleared her throat. "Well, we've had a few updates to our business plan." She glanced at her partner and shook her head, unable to hide her smile. "And we love the name Haven, so we aren't *For Women*, anymore."

"We are going to be *Haven House*," Carol announced breathlessly. "In honor of you."

Melody nodded her agreement. "And we may help a few unwed mothers, but our focus has shifted. We want to provide support to those in transition."

Candy shrugged. "You can't fight fate. You came here for a reason, and I know in my heart it was so we would know the direction we were meant to take."

Her mouth wide, Haven made the loop again, gaping at them. "Are you serious?" She stamped her foot, then squealed. Grabbing Candy, who still stood beside her, she wriggled wildly as the other girls joined them.

Once they had tired of the group hug, Haven dabbed her eyes and tried again. "Ok, I really have a toast. But I've lost my glass." She cast her gaze around, looking for it, before Roger placed it in her trembling hand.

"I thought you might drop it," he gruffly explained with a wink.

"Thanks. I probably would have." She held up the liquid and poured her feelings into her words. "To Haven House. And to the best group of friends and family a girl could ever have."

Epilogue

Standing shoulder to shoulder, a cool spring breeze buffeted the line of women. In somber reverence, they formed a small arch before a large, polished stone.

"It looks amazing," Carol praised, dabbing the corner of her eye.

Candy knelt, pressing her hand against the cold flat surface. "Yes. Gary insisted on it. I'm glad he did." She sniffed. "And really, I'm glad she was finally able to let go. I truly know she's at peace now."

"She held out for so long." Holly sputtered a muted laugh. "She was tough."

"Until the bitter end," Haven confirmed. "I'm glad I got to know her."

"You think she see us?" Bella asked, glancing at the others. "I hope that she does. I hope that she'll be proud."

"She's proud," Annette assured, giving her daughter a squeeze. "And yes, I'm sure she will watch over each and every one of us. Always."

"Indeed," Eveline whispered. Stepping forward, she

laid a single pink rose upon the freshly turned earth. "Goodbye, my sweet and dearest friend, Lanelle."

Thank You

Thank you for reading, and I hope that you have enjoyed the adventures of Gary, Candy and all the friends and family of the Sweet Christmas Series. Until we meet again, all my love. ~ Sam

Books in this series include:
Christmas Candy (2015)
Christmas Eve (2016)
Christmas Carol (2017)
Christmas Joy (2018)
Christmas Holly (2019)
Christmas Lane (2020)
Christmas Bell (2021)
Christmas Melody (2022)
Christmas Haven (2023)

About the Author

Anyone who knows me could tell you, I am a friendly kind of person, never met a stranger and take up conversations anywhere at any time. I work hard, and my mind never seems to shut down, as I wake up often in the middle of the night with ideas pouring out and demanding to be dealt with. Of course that means much of my books were written in the middle of the night.

I grew up and still live in the great state of Texas where everything is bigger, where we have warm weather and a central location. I love my state, my town, and my family, which includes my four sons, my significant other, and many friends as well.

I have thoroughly enjoyed writing this story and hope that you will love reading it just as much. And of course, there will be many more adventures to come.

You can follow Samantha Jacobey at:
Website: www.SamJacobey.com
Facebook: https://www.facebook.com/SamJacobey
Twitter: https://twitter.com/SamJacobey

Also by SAMANTHA JACOBEY

https://www.lavishpublishing.com/authors/samantha-jacobey/

A New Life Series – an epic adventure, TORI FARRELL's life IS one wild story... escaped from a biker gang and running from drug lords... used by the FBI and hoping to protect her present from her past... IT'S DARK - IT'S BRUTAL, and it's WORTH EVERY MINUTE OF IT!! (Mature read, 18+ for graphic sexual content and violence, including rape)

Summer Spirit Novella Series - no one EVER had a summer romance like this… Charlie visits another plane, parallel to our own, where Summer Angels and Dark Angels battle over the fate of man. A unique twist on an old idea that will keep you guessing; will Charlie and Clarisse ever find their HEA? (New adult)

Teach Me to Prey – in this standalone thriller, JASON TRUITT and his friends have gotten their way for years. Deceit, sex, and foul play aren't normally covered in the curriculum, but they're doing whatever it takes to get under BECKY STEWART's skin. When one of the boys turns up dead, it's a race against time to save the others; a STUNNING STORY that will get your heart racing and leave you breathless by the end… (New Adult)

The Binding (Unexpected Magic #1) - One cursed diary will change two strangers forever...Can Meri and Rider use her mother's old book to figure out why someone is after them? Or will the guilty party succeed, ripping the tome away before killing them and then slithering back into the darkness… (New Adult)

The Wicked Awakened (Unexpected Magic #2) – a Halloween novel; a five-hundred-year-old witch wants to turn SARAH MATTHEWS' body into her new home… A twisted tale involving a coven hell bent on seeing that she succeeds. Who will come out on top in this epic battle of wills? (Mature read, 18+ for graphic sexual content and violence)

The Irrevocable Series - From affluent beginnings, BAILEY DEWITT's life has become a broken mess... after her parents died unexpectedly, she didn't think it could get any worse. But when the arrogance of man catches up and puts the entire world into a dooms-day spiral, there will be only ONE PLACE she can run to - the ONE PLACE she wanted desperately to escape. (New Adult)

The Dragon of Eriden Series - Amicia Spicer led a simple life, until she discovered it had all been a lie… On her deathbed, Arely Spicer confessed to her only daughter that she had been found by, not born to her mother and father. Sad news to be certain, the idea of having a family of flesh and blood waiting to be reunited sent the young, independent woman on the adventure of a lifetime. Little did she know, a dragon's heart beat within her chest and her journey would be more perilous than she could have imagined... (New Adult)

Also from our Lavish family

Love on the Double Duo
By L.A. Remenicky
https://books2read.com/LoveDoubleDuo

The Monroe brothers fall fast, they fall hard, and they fall forever. But the road to true love isn't always easy.

Loving Jessie's Girl – Book 1: Until AJ Monroe left Indiana after college he had always lived in his identical twin brother's shadow. He had made a life for himself in Denver, Colorado, away from Jessie, away from Indiana. But when AJ feared for his brother's safety, he left everything behind to step back into the shadow he thought he had outgrown. Finding his brother was AJ's only concern...until he met Jessie's girl.

Fiercely independent, Rina Abbot hid her true situation from everyone, including her best friend, Jessie. Out of money and unable to care for her rescue dogs she had no choice but to accept the help of the handsome stranger with a familiar face. Afraid to trust him, she tried to ignore the feelings he stirred within her as they searched for his missing brother.

But secrets never stay secrets for long.

Finally open about their feelings for each other, Rina's secrets began to wreak havoc on their lives. Would Rina's secrets force AJ to give up his dream of loving Jessie's girl?

Beyond Duty − Book 2: After serving in the Marine Corps, Jessie Monroe has finally found a life beyond war. He's focused on

being an EMT and helping his best friend rescue dogs, until he happens upon a curvy blonde stranded

with a flat tire and no jack.

On the run from her past, Dori Graham is slow to trust any man, and she tries to ignore the spark of

interest she feels for her handsome savior, but a friendship grows between them.

When Dori's past invades her new life, Jessie vows to rescue her. Saving her will take him beyond duty

and into his own personal hell. Calling upon his training as a Marine and the depth of his feelings for

Dori, Jessie will need the mental strength to battle to save her and, ultimately, save himself.

Between the Trees
Kathy Moczerniak
https://www.lavishpublishing.com/authors/kathy-moczerniak/

A beautiful coming of age with a dark side that one teenager must fight to overcome…

Beyond Kathryn Lucas' first memory of her father's tree lay a dysfunctional path of violence, heartbreak, and secrets within a family severely entrenched in the vicious cycle of abuse. A lifetime of fear drives her from her home, and the teenage girl finds refuge with an aunt and uncle determined to protect their niece.

Distressing flashbacks unravel in Kathryn's fragile mind among the turmoil encircling her as she struggles through adolescence and descends into her pain-ridden past. When the summation of her unsettling memories allows the darkness to overtake her, she becomes desperate to unearth the light.

Inspired by a true story, Kathryn must hold on tightly to those who love her, searching for her place in a world threatening to break her as she fights to overcome life's betrayals before she is deprived of her future.

The Hunter Series
Sara J. Bernhardt
https://books2read.com/HuntersTrilogySet

Jane Callahan is a reclusive, seventeen-year-old high school student dealing with the death of her beloved brother. Her home in Southern California with her mother is a constant reminder of her loss and pain. In hopes of escaping her past she moves to North Bend Oregon to live with her father, where she meets a beautiful boy named Aidan Summers.

Jane is intrigued by his looks as well as his unusual ways of attempting to get her attention. After months of uncommon conversation and frustration, an uncertain romance brews between Jane and Aidan, but Aidan has a ghastly secret that could destroy everything.

www.ingramcontent.com/pod-product-compliance
Lightning Source LLC
Chambersburg PA
CBHW051301170626
46809CB00004B/1744